SORDID GAMES

ELIZABETH KELLY

EK PUBLISHING INC.

SORDID GAMES

Rudolph isn't the only one playing games this Christmas...

Daisy Morrison's plan for a quiet and perfectly dull Christmas isn't working out. Her roommate has a secret boyfriend and, terrified her family will find out, convinces Daisy to be her pretend lesbian lover during the holidays. Sleeping with a handsome and sexy stranger the night before she meets her "girlfriend's" family probably isn't Daisy's wisest idea. But it's only one night. What could go wrong?

Wes McKinley wasn't looking to hook up at the bar during the holidays. He just needed a night away from his crazy, well-meaning family. But when he meets Daisy, he can't resist her sweetness or the instant connection they have. Sleeping with a woman he barely knows isn't his usual thing, but it's only one night. What could go wrong?

When Wes and Daisy meet again in the last place they expected, Wes suspects she's playing games. But if he has his way, in the end, neither of them will lose...

CHAPTER 1

Daisy

"Laid off? But you were just hired six months ago."

"Yeah, I know." I collapsed on the couch with a harsh sigh and rubbed at my temples.

Frannie plopped down on the other end of the couch and grabbed my legs, pulling them into her lap before beginning to rub my feet. "I'm sorry, Daisy."

I groaned in pleasure and rested my head against the back of the couch as Frannie continued to rub my feet. I had only been roommates with the tiny, blonde woman for five months, but we were already best friends.

"Me too, Frannie. I really liked this job, you know? My patients were great, my boss was great, my coworkers were…"

I trailed off, and Frannie grinned at me. "Great?"

"Mostly," I said.

"There are other rehab facilities in the city, you'll find something," Frannie said.

"Yeah, but not this close to Christmas," I said as the front door slammed. Moments later, Frannie's boyfriend, Owen, sauntered into the room.

"Hey, sexy ladies, what's happening?"

He sat in the armchair across from us and winked at Frannie. She jumped up and hurried across the room to sit in his lap. They kissed deeply, and when Owen's hand began to inch up toward Frannie's boob, I said, "Keep it in your pants, buddy."

Owen laughed as Frannie blushed and gave me an apologetic look. "Sorry, sweetie."

"I can't help it. My lady is hot." Owen gave Frannie an appreciative look.

Despite my current jaded attitude toward love and men, I had to admit, it was kind of cute how crazy Owen and Frannie were for each other. Owen was good-looking, with his shaggy blond hair, blue eyes, and lean body, but I liked my men tall and big with dark hair. Nothing made me hotter than a strong jaw with the perfect amount of stubble. Of course, even if Owen had been Mr. Tall, Dark and Handsome, he was definitely not my type. His laid-back and easygoing nature was perfect for Frannie, but it left me cold.

"Why so sad looking, D?" Owen suddenly asked.

"She lost her job," Frannie said.

"Blows," Owen replied. "Sorry, dude."

"Thanks, Owen," I said.

"So, are you going to start looking for a job right away?" Frannie asked.

"No, I'll wait until January." I picked at a thread on my jeans. "It's like a week before Christmas. No one will be hiring over the holidays."

"So, now that you're not working, you have zero plans for the holidays," Frannie said.

I threw one of the couch pillows at her. "Way to make me sound like a complete loser, Frannie."

She didn't reply. She was staring at Owen, and he cocked an eyebrow at her. "What, babe?"

She pressed a kiss against his mouth before sliding off his lap and joining me on the couch again. "Daisy, why don't you come with me to my parents' place for Christmas?"

I shook my head. "That's very sweet, but I'm not intruding on your family time."

"Sweetie, I want you to come. Now that you and Dick have broken up, you'll be all alone at Christmas."

"One, his name was Richard, not Dick, and two, I've been alone at Christmas before. It's no big deal. I'll order Chinese food and do a Netflix marathon," I said.

"Or, you could come home with me and enjoy a traditional Christmas dinner, open presents with my family on Christmas morning and participate in all the holiday festivities around town. You might even meet someone."

Frannie wiggled her eyebrows at me, and I rolled my eyes. "I've taken a vow of celibacy, remember? I have no interest in meeting *someone*."

"Can you even be a nun if you've already had sex?" Owen said.

"A vow of celibacy doesn't automatically make you a nun, Owen," I replied as Frannie giggled.

"Fair enough," Owen said. "Hell, not even nuns are celibate anyway. I knew this chick once who was a nun, and she, like, banged two different guys at the same party."

"Oh my God," Frannie said, "that was a Halloween party, baby, and she was in a nun costume."

Owen squinted at her. "You sure?"

"Positive," Frannie replied.

"Fuck," Owen said, "I gotta cut back on the weed."

Both Frannie and I laughed, and Owen gave us a cheerful grin before pulling out his cell phone. He studied the screen as Frannie took my hands and squeezed them. "Seriously, sweetie. I think you should come with me. My parents have an extra room in the basement. Say you'll come with me…please?"

I studied her silently, noting the way her gaze didn't quite meet mine. "What's going on, Frannie?"

"Nothing." She darted a quick look at Owen. "Nothing's going on."

"Don't lie to me," I said. "Why are you suddenly so anxious for me to spend Christmas with you and your family?"

Frannie took a deep breath. "Okay, so, don't freak out, but I need to ask you a huge favour."

"What?"

"Now that you're not working and have no plans for the holidays, I want you to come home with me and pretend to be my girlfriend."

I blinked at her. "I – what?"

"Babe, that's brilliant," Owen said.

I gave him a look of confusion as Frannie said, "I want you to tell my family that you're my girlfriend and we're in a relationship."

"I know I swore off men, but I'm not switching teams. I'm practicing celibacy, not lesbianism," I said. "And spoiler alert – you're not a lesbian either."

"Damn straight," Owen said without looking up from his phone. He held his fist up and bumped the air as Frannie gave me a pleading look.

"Please, Daisy. Just help me out, okay?"

"No," I said. "No, definitely not. Why would your parents believe that we were lesbians? You've been dating Owen for a year."

"Well, they don't exactly know about Owen," Frannie said.

"What? How can they not?"

"It's kind of a long story," Frannie said.

"You just asked me to tell your family I'm your lesbian lover. I think you can sum up the long story for me," I said.

Frannie blew a lock of her blonde hair out of her face. "Okay, you know that Owen and I grew up in the same town, right?"

"Yes. Your families live next to each other."

"Right. So, years ago, my dad and Owen's dad were like stupid big rivals at their high school. They were both really popular and on the basketball team, but they totally hated each other's guts. They were constantly trying to outdo each other, and everything was one big competition between them. My mom said that even though he hated public speaking, my dad still joined the debate team just because Owen's dad did. Anyway, they still hate each other and growing up, I wasn't allowed to be friends with Owen or his sister, even though they lived right next door to us."

"Are you kidding me?" I said. "It's been like thirty years. They can't still be enemies over stupid high school shit."

"Dude, you don't know our dads," Owen said solemnly. "They're both stubborn as hell."

"Anyway, I barely even talked to Owen when we were kids. I didn't even know he'd moved away from Darville until I bumped into him here," Frannie said. "We started talking and I realized that he was really a pretty cool guy, and then we..."

"Then we started boning," Owen said.

"Owen!"

"What? It's true, babe. You can't keep your hands off this." He lifted his shirt and rubbed his admittedly impressive looking six pack.

Frannie rolled her eyes. "Anyway, Owen is going home for Christmas too, and we thought we were going to tell them then. But Owen's dad wants this historical home torn down to make room for new townhouses. So, the Darville Historical Society got involved in saving and restoring it."

"What does that have to do with anything?" I said.

"My dad is the president of the Darville Historical Society," Frannie said.

"Oh," I replied.

"Dude, my dad, like, hates history and stuff." Owen stared at his cell phone again.

"We can't tell them right now, Daisy," Frannie said. "It'll make everything worse."

"Okay, fine, I get that," I said. "But I don't understand why you need me to pretend to be your girlfriend. Just pretend to be single."

"Yeah, see, my parents really want grandchildren," Frannie said. "Now that they think I've been single for over a year, my mom and my grandma have already made it clear that they're going to try and set me up with half the damn town over Christmas. We've got a lot of single guys in Darville, Daisy. I don't want to spend my entire holiday fending them off."

"What about your brother?" I said.

"Dude, she can't pretend to date her brother. That's disgusting," Owen said.

"Shut up, Owen," I said. "Your brother is older than you, right? You said he's flying in for Christmas, too. Maybe you can convince your mom and grandma to try and set him up instead."

Frannie shook her head. "It won't work. My brother is immune to Mom's guilt trips about not giving her grandkids."

"You can't spend the rest of your life pretending to be a lesbian. Sooner or later, you and Owen will get married and then what?"

"We're going to tell them once the holidays are over and

this stupid historical house thing is done. When things are a bit calmer, and our fathers only hate each other the usual amount, then we'll tell them."

"But they'll think you're a lesbian!" I nearly shouted.

"I'll tell them I'm bisexual," Frannie said. "We are going to tell them. Just not right now."

"I don't think I can pretend to be a lesbian," I said. "I love you, Frannie, but I'm not, I mean..."

"You don't give her a lady boner, babe."

"Owen!" Frannie turned toward me again. "Sweetie, my parents are super conservative. Honestly, it's going to freak them out when I tell them we're dating. They probably won't let us share the same bedroom. At the most, we'll have to do a bit of handholding, maybe kiss once or twice."

"If there's tongue, make sure you get a picture," Owen said.

"No tongue," Frannie said. "Only a quick, close-mouthed kiss once or twice to sell the relationship."

"You should still get a picture," Owen said.

"Please, Daisy," Frannie said.

I hesitated, and Owen glanced up from his cell phone. "Babe, if Daisy really doesn't want to do it, we shouldn't make her."

Frannie gave him a look of frustration. "Baby, if my parents believe I'm a lesbian for a few months and then I tell them that I'm dating you, it'll work in our favour. They'll probably be so relieved I'm not a lesbian that they'll be happy we're dating."

"You'd do that to your own family?" I said.

"It's a good lesson for them," Frannie said.

"Wait," Owen said. "Dude, are you telling me that your parents will only think I'm good enough for you because I got a penis instead of a vagina?"

"Possibly," Frannie said.

Owen considered that for a moment before grinning. "Harsh, but fair."

"Frannie, I don't know," I said.

"C'mon," Frannie pleaded, "I don't like the idea of you spending Christmas all alone, and I really need your help with this. Please, Oopsie?"

I could feel myself caving when she said her nickname for me. Shortly after we became roommates, Frannie and I went out to a bar together. Long story short, we drank too much and I bit the pavement outside the bar, falling flat on my face. When Frannie had rolled me onto my back, asking frantically if I was hurt, I had grinned and mumbled, "Oopsie-Daisy".

She'd burst into laughter before falling next to me. We had giggled hysterically until the bouncer came out, picked us both up and pushed us into a cab. That night cemented our friendship.

"Fine, I'll do it," I said, "but you seriously owe me for this, Frannie."

Frannie squealed and threw her arms around me. She hugged me before kissing my cheek. "Thank you, Daisy. You have no idea how much you're helping us."

CHAPTER 2

Daisy

"Why are we stopping at a motel? I thought we were staying with your parents?" I stared out the windshield at the glowing neon sign of the motel.

"Well," Frannie said as I shut the car off, "technically we're not supposed to be at my parents' house until tomorrow."

"Then why did we leave today?" There was a knock on my window, and I screamed and jumped, banging the top of my head against the top of the car. "Ouch! Goddammit, Owen!"

"Sorry, dude," Owen said cheerfully as Frannie climbed out of the car and ran around to my side. She hugged Owen before kissing him.

"I missed you, baby."

"Missed you too, babe." Owen kissed her again.

"It's been two days since you saw him last." I climbed out of the car.

"It's been hell without you," Frannie said. "I hate being apart from you."

"Well, get used to it," I said a bit irritably. "You're a lesbian starting now, for the next week, remember?"

"Starting tomorrow," Owen said. "Pop the trunk and I'll get your bags."

"Wait? You're staying here tonight, too?" I asked.

He nodded as Frannie popped the trunk and said, "I booked a couple of rooms at the motel for tonight. I thought maybe once we were settled, I could slip over to Owen's room and we'd have one last night of - "

"Boning." Owen walked over to us, carrying both my suitcase and Frannie's.

"So, I'm supposed to hang out in the motel room by myself all night?" I said. "Way to treat your pretend lesbian lover, Frannie."

"I'm sorry, sweetie, but this is my last night with Owen."

"For a week," I said. "You seriously can't go a week without having sex with him?"

"I'm really good at boning," Owen said.

"I just want one more night with my baby," Frannie said. "There's a bar not far from here. You can go have a drink, maybe meet someone."

"Won't your parents wonder where you are?" I asked Owen.

"Nah, I told them I was gonna chill with my bros tonight." Owen shifted the suitcases in his hands.

"What happens when someone sees you with Owen?" I said to Frannie. "The lesbian lover story will be blown before it even starts."

"No one is going to see us," Frannie said. "The motel is a good ten miles outside of town, and besides, technically I'm staying in your room with you."

"You just made out with Owen in the parking lot," I said. "He's carrying our suitcases for God's sake!"

"I'm a gentleman," Owen said.

"No one saw us making out," Frannie said. "One last night, Daisy. Go to the bar, have a drink and relax. Enjoy your alone time, okay? Starting tomorrow, we'll be smothered by my family."

"You didn't mention the smothering when you talked me into this crazy idea," I muttered.

"Maybe smothering isn't the right word, more like really intense mothering," Frannie said.

"Fantastic." I grabbed my suitcase from Owen and, walking carefully on the snow-covered ground, started toward the lobby of the motel.

* * *

Wes

I WANTED HER THE MOMENT I SAW HER. I'D BEEN SITTING IN the bar for nearly two hours, nursing my beer and people watching, when she walked in, shrugged out of her thick jacket and sat down at the long, curved bar. I didn't recognize her, but that wasn't surprising. The bar was outside of town, and I wondered briefly if I had chosen this one because I was deliberately avoiding old friends.

Of course, if the woman sitting at the bar and sipping a glass of wine had lived in Darville when I was growing up, I may never have left. She was wearing skinny jeans with a dark red long-sleeved shirt that hugged her breasts. Despite her slender build, she had to be a C cup, maybe a D. They looked firm and perky through her shirt, and I was suddenly itching to touch them. Her light brown hair brushed against her shoulders, and I wondered if it was as soft as it looked.

She lifted her wine glass and took a drink. Her back was to me, so I couldn't see her face, but I remembered it easily enough from her short walk to the bar. Pale skin, cute little button nose, perfect pink lips and gorgeous blue eyes. I studied her hand as she drummed her fingers restlessly against the gleaming wood of the bar. She had long fingers, and I wondered idly what they would look like wrapped around my dick.

For a moment, I was tempted to stand up from my table in the corner, cross the bar and ease onto the stool beside her. It'd been a while since I'd gotten laid, and the woman was hitting all of my buttons. Hell, I had half a stiffy just from staring at the back of her damn head. Before I could even try to hit on her, another man sat down next to her. A weird little trickle of possessiveness went down my back, and I shook it off. What the hell was wrong with me? I didn't even know the woman. I forced myself to look at the TV mounted in the far corner. I wasn't here to get laid. I was here to spend time with my family at Christmas.

Of course, that didn't stop me from glancing over at the woman every five minutes for the next half-hour. I couldn't hear what the guy sitting next to her was saying, but it was obvious she was blowing him off. He either didn't get it or didn't want to take the hint. I watched with growing irritation as he continued to hit on her. She wasn't mine, I didn't even know her damn name, but I was instantly angry when the guy dropped his arm around her shoulders and pulled her up against him. When she tried to pull away and he refused to let her, I was on my feet and headed toward them without a second thought.

Daisy

I WAS STARTING TO REGRET COMING TO THE BAR. I SHOULD have stayed in my motel room and watched *The Bachelor* instead. The guy sitting next to me for the last half hour was an asshole who was totally ignoring my 'fuck off' signals. I took another big gulp of my wine and waved at the bartender for the bill. She ignored me as she flirted with a big lumberjack looking fellow at the far end of the bar. I sighed and rubbed at my forehead.

"So, what did you say your name was again, hot thing?"

I rolled my eyes and tried not to wince. The guy sitting beside me was good looking enough, but he was already halfway plastered, and his breath could have knocked over a dragon.

"I didn't," I said. "Listen, you're not picking up on my very obvious body language, so I'm going to straight up tell you that I'm not interested in you. Go away."

The man didn't blink an eye, and I made a soft squeak of surprise when he dropped one heavy arm around my shoulders and yanked me closer. "C'mon, don't be like that."

"Let me go," I said before trying to pull away.

He held me tighter, his arm a band of steel around me, and fear trickled down my spine. I shook it off. I was in a public place, surrounded by plenty of people.

"Let me go before I kick you in the nuts," I said.

"I hate women with smart mouths, you know that?" He was slurring his words a little, and I couldn't help cringing when his fingers dug into my arm. "And you seem to have a real smart mouth, don't ya?"

"Fuck you," I said. "Let go of me now or - "

"Sorry, I'm late, honey. I got caught up at work."

I turned my head toward the low, raspy voice coming from my left side. The man of my goddamn dreams was standing next to me, and it was all I could do to keep my mouth from dropping open. I stared up at him as he leaned against the bar and cocked one eyebrow at me. His eyes were the colour of dark chocolate, and he had a perfect nose and perfect lips and a faint indent in his chin that I suddenly wanted to touch. With my tongue. Dark stubble covered his square jaw, and my nipples beaded into hard points. How would it feel to have that stubble rubbing against them? Me and my nipples wanted to find out. Immediately.

He was well over six feet with broad shoulders and a narrow waist, and what I was sure would be a perfect damn ass, clad in stupidly tight jeans. I stared briefly at his package, my cheeks reddening when I lifted my gaze to his, and there was amusement in his eyes.

My lust-fogged brain finally clued in that he was speaking, and I stuttered, "W-what?"

"I asked who your new friend was." He stared around me and gave the man a tight grin. "You might want to take your hand off my woman."

I heard the audible click of his throat as the drunk man swallowed, and the heavy weight of his arm disappeared. I didn't object when my dream man put his arm around my waist. In fact, I leaned forward and eagerly tilted my head up toward him. I wanted this utterly perfect stranger to kiss me.

He didn't disappoint. His head dipped down, and I closed my eyes as his warm, firm lips brushed against mine. I returned his kiss with an embarrassing amount of enthusiasm. I parted my lips and made a soft whimper of pleasure when he briefly dipped his tongue between them to touch mine. The whimper turned into a moan of disappointment when he lifted his head.

He stared pointedly at the man sitting on the other side of me. "You should go now."

The man stumbled away, and some of my common sense returned when the stranger let go of my waist and sat on the stool next to me. I stared at my almost empty glass of wine and tried to control my runaway heartbeat. What the hell was happening to me? Pretend lesbian relationship aside, I was done with men for at least the next ten years. Celibacy. Celibacy was what I both wanted and needed.

"You okay?"

His deep voice made butterflies flicker to life in my stomach. Hell, butterflies? I had a goddamn gymnastic team practicing their tumbling routine in there.

"Yes, thank you," I said. "I appreciate the help."

He shrugged. "You seemed to have it under control, but sometimes the pretend boyfriend routine is easier and cleaner than the kick them in the balls route. No one likes to see a grown man burst into tears and vomit simultaneously."

I laughed. "I suppose not. I'm Daisy, by the way."

"Wes." He held out his big hand, and I hesitated briefly before shaking it. Immediately, the gymnasts in my stomach broke out into synchronized cartwheels. Shit, I was in trouble if just the touch of his hand made me want to drag him back to my motel room.

I realized I was still holding his hand and dropped it with a muttered apology. He smiled at me and waved at the bartender, who immediately came over.

"Well, hey, Sugar. What can I get you?" she purred.

"I'll take whatever you have on tap and whatever the lady would like."

"I'll have another glass of wine, please," I said.

She nodded and hurried away as I smiled at Wes. "Thank you."

"You're welcome." He smiled again at me before saying, "So, in the interest of not getting my ass kicked – do you have a boyfriend?"

I shook my head. "No. Do you have a girlfriend?"

"Would you be surprised to know I'm single?" he asked with a flirty grin.

"Shocked, actually."

"Is it because of my good looks or my charming personality?"

"Probably a little of both."

"Good to know," he said as the bartender returned with our drinks. He took a drink of beer as I sipped at my new glass of wine.

"Do you live around here?" I asked.

"Used to," he said. "I'm home for the holidays. How about you?"

"No. I came here with a friend," I said.

There was a bit of awkward silence, and I tried frantically to think of something witty to say. Oh God, why did I have to suck so hard at flirting? And why the hell did Wes have to smell so good? It was short-circuiting my ability to think straight.

I took another sip of wine.

You've got this, Daisy. It's just a beautiful guy whom you have no interest in sleeping with because you've taken a vow of celibacy. You don't need to flirt with him. Just say something cool, for God's sake.

I took a deep breath and said, "So, uh, what's a nice guy like you doing in a place like this?"

He laughed, and I did a face plant into the palm of my hand.

"Isn't that supposed to be my line?" He teased.

"Sorry," I said. "I have no idea why I said that. I can't sleep with you - I've taken a vow of celibacy."

Wes choked on his swallow of beer, and with my face flaming red, I pounded him on the back as he coughed repeatedly.

"Shit! I'm sorry! I don't know why I told you that – forget I said it!" I smacked him on the back again and gave him an anxious look as he wiped his hand across his mouth. "Are you okay?"

"Yeah, thanks," he said.

"Good, I'm really sorry."

"It's fine," he said.

I waited a beat and said, "Is there any chance you'll forget the celibacy thing?"

"Not a chance."

My groan of dismay made him grin before he leaned a little closer. "So, any particular reason you've taken a vow of celibacy?"

"Six months ago, my boyfriend and I broke up. It was amicable enough, we just wanted different things, you know?"

Wes nodded and took another drink of beer.

"I decided to try online dating."

"Uh oh," Wes said.

I laughed. "Yeah. I went on first dates with five different men over a period of six weeks. All of them were terrible, and the third and fifth ones bordered on complete disasters."

"How disastrous?" Wes asked.

"The third one told me he was a musician."

"You don't look like someone who dates musicians," Wes said.

I shrugged. "He wasn't a musician, really. Unless you think playing gigs at the local seniors' home for free makes a thirty-year-old man a musician?"

He roared with laughter, and I flushed with pleasure at the sound of it.

"Wow, he told you this on the first date?"

"Oh no. Our date was at the seniors' home. He thought I would enjoy watching the way he 'worked a crowd'."

"You're joking."

"I wish I were," I said. "But to be fair, some of those seniors really got into it. An old lady at the front threw underwear at him."

Wes nearly howled with laughter as I said, "Mind you, they belonged to the guy sitting next to her, but I overheard him telling the nurse she threw farther than him."

"Holy shit." Wes wiped at his eyes. "I can't believe that's a true story."

"It is. The fifth one was worse."

"It can't be."

"He brought his mom on the date."

"Do you live in a sitcom?" Wes asked. "Is that what's happening?"

"Trust me, there was no laugh track for this date."

"What did you do?" Wes asked.

I shrugged. "I had dinner with him and his mom. At the end of the date, he walked me to my car. His mom stood at their car and shouted across the parking lot not to kiss me. That she could tell I had the sex disease."

Wes' mouth dropped open, and I laughed and said, "I can assure you that she was wrong. I don't have the sex disease."

Wes laughed again. "That's crazy."

"Yeah, now you know why I took a vow of celibacy. Five online dates in six weeks were more than enough to convince me that celibacy was the way to go."

"Fair enough," he said.

"What about you? Why are you single?" I took another sip of wine and tried to look like I wasn't about five minutes away from sticking my hand down his deliciously tight jeans.

"The cliché of being too busy with my career, I suppose," he said. "I've dated on and off for the last few years, but nothing serious."

"What do you do for a living?"

"Engineer."

"My dad was an engineer," I said.

"Is he still one?"

"He and my mom passed away a few years ago. Rainy night, bad brakes on their car."

He reached out and squeezed my hand. "I'm sorry."

"Thank you. It's still hard, especially around their birthdays and the holidays, but I've done lots of grief counseling and have a few excellent support groups that I belong to." I smiled at him. He held my hand a moment longer, and I shivered all over when he rubbed his thumb over the palm of my hand before letting go.

"What do you do for a living?" he asked.

"Rehabilitation therapist," I replied.

"Do you like it?"

"I do. I like helping people. Do you like your job?"

"Yes. I work for a smaller company, and we have good clients."

"That's great." I studied the stubble that surrounded his mouth and wondered how it would feel against my inner thighs.

"Shit."

I jerked at Wes's low mutter and said, "What's wrong?"

"I'm sorry. I need to go." He pulled out his wallet and placed some bills on the bar.

Disappointment coursed through me. "Oh, yeah. Of course. Okay. It was nice to meet you."

I held out my hand, and Wes stared at it for a moment before stepping closer. He ignored my hand and cupped my face, staring intently at me as his thumb rubbed across my cheekbone.

"Let me make something clear, Daisy. I don't want to leave. You're beautiful and sexy as hell, but if I stay any longer, I'll do something stupid."

"Like what?" I whispered.

"Like telling you that I want to fuck you until you forget all about your goddamn vow of celibacy."

I shivered all over and stared wide-eyed at him as he studied my mouth. For a moment, I thought he was going to kiss me, but instead he lifted my hand to his mouth and pressed a kiss against my knuckles. The scrape of his stubble sent a new wave of lust through my body, and I swallowed heavily as he gave me a look of regret.

"Instead, for once in my life, I'm going to do the right thing. It was a pleasure to meet you, Daisy."

He kissed my knuckles again, and I watched in numb disbelief as he walked out of the bar.

Wes

"You fucking idiot," I muttered to myself as I unlocked the truck. "You're lucky she didn't slap you across the face when you said you wanted to fuck her."

I yanked the door open, but froze when I heard my name called. I turned around. Daisy was hurrying toward me.

"Wes, wait a minute, I – shit!"

Her feet slipped on the icy pavement, and she pinwheeled her arms madly as I lunged forward. My own feet slipped out from under me as I grabbed her around the waist and we fell to the ground with a heavy thud. I twisted as we fell and cushioned Daisy's body with my own. Her soft and curvy body felt way too good on top of mine, even with most of it hidden by a thick winter jacket. I stayed on the ground, holding her tightly against me despite the coldness of the pavement under me.

"Wes! Oh my God, are you okay?"

She tried to scramble off of me, and I held her a little tighter as I stared at her mouth. I had kissed that mouth, felt the softness of her lips and tasted the sweetness of her tongue. My cock hardened in my jeans, and without thinking, I shifted her against me so her pussy was pressed up against it.

Her eyes widened, and she licked her bottom lip. I groaned and cupped the back of her head, pulling her down until her lips met mine. I immediately took control of the kiss, threading my fingers through her soft hair as I angled my mouth over hers and thrust my tongue into her mouth. She sucked at it, and I groaned again and rubbed my dick against her.

Her sweet little moan set my blood on fire, but I pulled her head back and stared at her swollen mouth with regret before easing her off of me and climbing to my feet. I took her hands and helped her stand.

"Sorry," I muttered. "I shouldn't have done that. Are you okay?"

"I'm fine," she said. "Are you? You were the one who actually hit the ground. Did you smack your head?"

"No."

She stared at me, and I cleared my throat before stepping back. "I gotta go."

I reached for the door of my truck, hesitating when she said, "Wes, wait!"

Sighing, I turned around. She was closer than I thought, so close I could smell her perfume and feel the brush of her winter jacket against my abdomen. "Daisy, I - "

"What if I want that too?"

"Want what?" I asked in confusion.

Her cheeks turned pink, but she took a deep breath and said, "What if I want to be fucked into forgetting about my vow of celibacy?"

My dick reacted to her words, growing so goddamn hard that I was certain an imprint of my zipper would be on it. I ignored my urge to yank her into my arms and instead said, "I'm staying at my mom and dad's house."

What the fuck?

Her mouth dropped open, and it was my turn to blush when she started to giggle.

"Shit," I said. "I meant that fucking a woman in my childhood bedroom with my parents down the hall isn't exactly dignified for a thirty-two-year-old man."

She laughed again. "Lucky for you, I have a motel room. It's nothing special but..."

She gave me an uncertain look. I slid my arm around her waist and pulled her nice and close, letting her feel the hardness of my dick. I bent my head and nuzzled her throat, liking the way she moaned and lifted her head to give me better access. "Are you sure this is what you want?"

"Yes," she said. "But, Wes, I – don't take this the wrong way, but I'm not, um, looking for anything more than tonight. Okay?"

I lifted my head and kissed the tip of her nose. "Okay."

"Are you sure?" she said anxiously. "You understand that I don't want anything but sex?"

I couldn't help but laugh. "Yes, I'm sure, and yes, I understand you only want sex."

She blushed again. "Sorry, I sound like I'm full of myself. I'm not assuming you want anything more than sex with me, it's just – I've never done anything like this before, so I'm not really sure how the, uh, rules work."

"I haven't done this before either, but I don't think there's a set of rules to follow for a one-night stand," I said.

"Right," she said, "of course. So, uh, did you want to follow me back to the motel?"

I nodded immediately. "Yes, I do."

CHAPTER 3

Daisy

I was nervous. I didn't want to be. I wanted to look sexy and confident, but the way my hand shook when I tried to insert the card key into the lock didn't exactly scream confidence. Wes's big hand covered mine, and he helped me insert the card into the slot. The red light turned green, and I opened the door before stepping out of the cold air and into the room. As I fumbled for the light, I had a sudden dismaying thought. What if Frannie were here? What if she had finished with Owen and was sleeping in the second double bed?

She won't be. She's spending the night with Owen, and you know that, you goober. Relax, for God's sake. Just because you're about to get naked and have sex with the perfect man doesn't mean you have to act like a complete idiot.

I took a deep breath. My inner voice was right. Besides, maybe Wes was good looking and funny and smart. And maybe the little dimple that showed up in his right cheek

every time he smiled at me made me nearly drip with anticipation. But he wasn't perfect. No one was.

He looks perfect.

He looked perfect, but he wasn't. He probably had, I don't
know, a small dick. I seized on that thought almost desperately. Yes, he probably had a small dick and was terrible in
bed. He probably sucked at sex, and it would be awkward
and weird, and my first one-night stand would be a complete
bust.

"Daisy?"

I realized we were still standing in the doorway in the
dark, and I hurriedly found the switch and flipped it on. Both
double beds were empty, and I took a deep breath before
turning to smile at Wes. "Sorry."

He studied me carefully. The door was still open, and a
chill was creeping into the room.

"Are you going to shut the door?" I crossed my arms
nervously over my torso.

"If you've changed your mind, I can leave."

I blinked at him. "I haven't changed my mind. Have you?"

"No, but you look nervous."

"I am nervous," I admitted.

"Don't be." He shut the door and locked it before taking
off his boots. I kicked mine off and held my hand out for his
jacket. He handed it to me, and I tossed both our jackets onto
Frannie's bed.

"Easy for you to say," I said. "You're really handsome and
have the perfect body, so…"

I studied the cheap carpet under my feet. What was
wrong with me? I usually had more self-confidence than this
in bed. Of course, I hadn't been with anyone but Richard in
the last two and a half years. Richard was used to the scar on
my tummy from my appendectomy, my weirdly long toes,
and the –

I suddenly froze and gave Wes a look of panic. "Oh shit."

"What?" He was reaching for me, and he stopped immediately. "What's wrong?"

"I haven't shaved."

He laughed. "I haven't shaved either."

"You don't understand," I said. "I haven't shaved in *weeks*. We're at Sasquatch levels of hair."

"I really don't care if your legs aren't shaved, Daisy. I swear." Wes reached down and adjusted the prominent bulge at the front of his jeans. "Let me show you how much I don't care."

"It's not just my legs." I glanced at my crotch. "I haven't exactly kept up with my waxing routine since I've been single."

Wes followed my gaze to my crotch, and I turned bright red. "You know what? Let's turn the lights off."

"Are you kidding me?" Wes said teasingly. "You can't tell me something like that and then expect me not to look."

"No way," I said. "I want the lights off and both of us under the covers."

Wes grabbed my hand before I could shut off the lights. "Sorry, darlin', but that's not happening." He pulled me into his arms and kissed me until I was clinging to him and panting. He kissed his way to my ear and sucked on my earlobe. "I want to see every inch of your tight little body tonight."

"Oh God," I moaned. "I could have a quick shower first. My razor is, like, right in my bag, give me ten minutes and – aah!"

Wes picked me up and carried me to the bed, dropping me onto it before stripping off his shirt. I sucked in my breath and stared hungrily at his broad chest and wide shoulders. A layer of dark hair covered his upper chest and arrowed down in a thin line below his belly button. Unsurprisingly, he had a six-pack, and I licked my lips and rose on my elbows as he reached for the button on his jeans.

"Crap! I don't have a condom!" I said as he flicked open the button. He grinned at me and reached into his back pocket for his wallet before bringing out the foil package and placing it on the nightstand.

"Thank God," I muttered. He stood gracefully on one foot and removed his sock before switching legs and removing the other.

He hesitated at the zipper, and I waved my hand at him. "Hey, no stopping now. You're just getting to the really good part."

He laughed and, with one agile movement, pushed his jeans and briefs down his legs and stepped out of them. I stared at the biggest, hardest dick I'd ever seen and tried not to drool.

"Oh no."

"Not the reaction I like to hear when I take off my pants."

I shook my head. "You really do have the perfect body."

"I don't."

"You do. I told myself that you probably had a small dick, but you don't. You really, really don't."

He gave me an arrogant little grin. "No, I really, really don't."

"Your self-confidence is not at all annoying or – oh!"

Wes had grabbed my feet, and he quickly peeled my socks off before tossing them on the floor. "Your turn, Daisy."

I took a deep breath and sat up before reaching for the hem of my shirt. "Okay, but try to remember that I wasn't expecting to sleep with someone tonight, so no judgment for my mismatched underwear. Okay?"

"If it helps, I'm not planning on you wearing it long enough for me to notice it doesn't match." Wes was still standing next to the bed without a lick of clothing or shame. When I glanced at his dick, he reached down and rubbed it.

Watching his rough hand rub his own dick made me drip into my panties, and I quickly stripped off my shirt before unbuttoning and unzipping my jeans. Wes released his cock and reached for my jeans, helping me tug the tight material down my legs.

He added them to the growing pile of clothes on the floor before reaching for my calf. I tried to pull my legs away, and with a sexy little growl, he cupped both my calves and pulled me closer. He rubbed his hands over my hairy shins as I closed my eyes and tried not to die of embarrassment. "I told you - Sasquatch levels."

"I like it," he said with a little grin before lying on his side on the bed beside me. He traced his finger over the front clasp of my bra. "May I?"

"Yes, please."

He unclasped it and pulled back the cups. When he inhaled sharply, I glanced at his face and blushed at the look of pure lust on his face.

"Wes, I - "

"So beautiful," he growled before cupping my left breast. He teased the nipple with his thumb, making a noise of approval when it hardened. He tugged on it before kneading my breast. I arched into his touch, and he kissed me softly on the mouth.

"Beautiful and perfect," he whispered against my lips before bending his head and sucking my nipple into his mouth.

I moaned and arched again, clutching at his head as he teased and toyed with both of my nipples until I was panting and shamelessly begging. He lifted his head and grinned at me. "Do you have any fucking idea how hot you are, Daisy?"

I tugged his head up until I could kiss him. We kissed repeatedly, our tongues flicking, tasting, and licking. I reached down and wrapped my fingers around his cock, marveling at the hard steel covered with velvet soft skin. I rubbed him lightly, smiling when he groaned and thrust into my hand.

"Fuck, that feels so good," he moaned.

I crowded closer, rubbing my nipples against the rough hair on his chest before licking and nibbling at his thick neck. He tasted delicious, and I bit him on the collarbone. He jerked against me, and I squeezed his dick before rubbing hard.

"Oh fuck," he muttered before pulling my hand away and pushing me onto my back.

"Hey," I said with a small pout. "I wasn't done yet."

"It's my turn," he said.

The tone of his voice brought fresh wetness to the crotch of my panties, and I shivered against him as he reached for the waistband of my panties. "Hips up, flower girl."

"Let's shut the lights off first."

"No," he said. "You're worrying for nothing, darlin'. I prefer the natural look, I promise."

"It's definitely natural," I muttered. I closed my eyes and lifted my hips. Wes pulled my underwear off and dropped them on the floor. There was silence, and I opened one eye.

"Wes? Are you horrified into silence or – oh my God!"

Wes pushed my knees apart and bent his head. He pressed a kiss against the curls at the top of my pussy as his fingers stroked my wet pussy lips. "So wet," he said appreciatively.

I tried not to hump his hand like a horny dog as he kissed the scar on my stomach. "What's this from?"

"App-appendectomy – oh my God, oh fuck…"

Wes had slid one thick finger into me, and I couldn't stop my hips from thrusting up. He lay down next to me again

28

and propped his head up in his free hand as he grinned at me. "I love your greedy little pussy, darlin'."

I blushed bright red, but his words made me squeeze around his finger. He groaned and brushed his mouth against mine. "I can't wait to feel you squeeze like that around my dick."

"Me either," I moaned. "Grab that condom."

He shook his head. "Not yet, little flower. I want to watch you come all over my fingers first."

I immediately tensed. "So, don't take this personally because this is my issue, not yours, but it's difficult to make me come. I usually need to do it myself."

He studied me silently, and I said, "I'm sorry. I swear it isn't you."

"Don't apologize," he said. "You have nothing to apologize for, but," he leaned down and kissed me as he pressed his thumb against my clit, "would you let me try?"

I gave him a cautious look. "I don't want you to be upset with me when it doesn't work."

"I won't be upset."

"You say that now, but when it doesn't work…"

Anxiety replaced the lust in my belly.

A flicker of anger crossed his face. "Did your ex get upset?"

"Sometimes."

He rubbed my clit with his thumb before kissing and nuzzling my neck. "I promise I won't get upset, Daisy. In fact, why don't you show me how you like to be touched?"

He pulled his finger from my pussy and reached for my hand, guiding it to my clit. "Show me," he whispered.

I rubbed at my clit as he watched. He was watching me with such intensity that I felt a little self-conscious. I wasn't sure I would come even by my own hand, but when he bent his head to my breast and sucked on my nipple, a new wave of lust rolled through me. I moaned softly and concentrated on touching my clit while his warm mouth worked my nipple into a hard bud.

When Wes pushed two thick fingers back into my throbbing pussy, my eyes popped open and I cried out with surprise and pleasure. He had released my nipple and was staring at my hand between my legs. I ground my pussy against his hand, my fingers rubbing my clit frantically.

"Good girl," he said in a low voice. "Rub your pretty little clit for me while I fuck you with my fingers."

The rough need in his voice, the firm thrust of his fingers, sent my lust spiraling out of control. Panting and moaning, I rubbed at my clit as he watched closely. I made a sharp cry, gave my clit one final hard, little pinch, and my orgasm burst inside of me in a sweet and almost overwhelming flood of pleasure. I shook wildly, my pussy clenching and unclenching around Wes's fingers as he bent his head again and kissed one hard nipple.

"So beautiful," he murmured.

I lay on the bed in a daze as he slowly eased his fingers out of me and then sat up. He grabbed the condom and quickly rolled it onto his cock before lying on his back beside me.

"Wes, that was really good," I breathed.

He grinned at me. "I'm glad. Climb on top of me, Daisy."

My legs felt like wet noodles, but I did what he asked. I straddled him, grabbed the base of his cock and guided it in. He groaned loudly but stayed perfectly still as I slowly sank onto his thick length.

"Good?" he asked.

I nodded. Wes was bigger than I was used to, but his thickness felt amazing as I stretched around him. "Yeah, so good."

I braced my hands on his broad chest and did a few

experimental bounces. He groaned, and his fingers dug into my hips as he stared hungrily at my breasts. "Your tits are amazing."

I grinned at him. "Thank you."

"Touch them," he demanded.

I cupped both of them, pulling on my nipples as Wes watched. I gasped when he grabbed my ass and made two hard thrusts. He groaned again. "Fuck, you're so goddamn tight."

Bracing my hands on his chest again, I met each of his strokes, using my knees for balance as I rose up and down. Wes's low groans of pleasure and his hard hands cupping and squeezing my ass made my swollen clit throb. I was reaching to touch it again – multiple orgasms weren't my thing, but Wes had me so hot, I figured it was worth a try – when Wes let go of my ass with his right hand and moved it to my pussy. He caressed my swollen and wet lips before rubbing my clit with the pads of his fingers.

I moaned encouragingly and dug my fingers into his chest as I rode him with hard, long strokes. I loved the roughness of Wes's fingers. They were so different from my soft skin, but he was touching me too gently. I needed a firmer touch, needed him to move a little to the left…

Without thinking, I grabbed his hand and moved it slightly before pressing hard on his hand and moving his fingers in firm circles against my clit. It felt incredible, and I cried out happily before rocking back and forth against his hand as I continued to move his fingers the way I wanted.

"Does that feel good, darlin'?" Wes panted.

I froze against him and then yanked my hand away from his. Richard had always hated it when I grabbed his hand, said it made him feel useless and incompetent.

I gave Wes a nervous look as I perched completely still on

top of him. "I'm sorry. I shouldn't have done that. You're doing a great job at touching me, really."

He laughed, and I moaned a little when it made his cock rub against my inner walls. "It's not that I don't appreciate the pep talk, but can we get back to the fucking? You do whatever feels good and makes you come all over my cock."

"I – are you sure?" I asked.

An almost painful look of need flickered across his face, and he gave my clit a rough pinch that made me squeal with pleasure and clench around his dick.

"Fuck! Yes, I'm sure!" he muttered.

I pressed my hand over his again and moved his fingers against my clit. His left hand was still cupping my ass, and I leaned back a little into his grip before letting my head fall back. I wanted to come again, wanted it desperately, and I closed my eyes and concentrated. Vaguely, I was aware of the way Wes pushed in and out of me with slow, rhythmic strokes, as I manipulated his fingers against my clit. The feel of his hard cock filling me up, the roughness of his fingers against that throbbing bundle of nerves, made me nearly weak with desire.

When Wes squeezed my clit between his fingers and gave it a sharp tug, my orgasm hit me as hard as a runaway train. I screamed, my back bowing and my nails digging into Wes' chest and wrist as the overwhelming intensity of my orgasm consumed me. I'd never had such a powerful orgasm before, and my pussy squeezed Wes's cock in a vice grip.

He made a low moan and then muttered a curse under his breath before shaking free of my grip and grabbing my hips with both of his hands. He pumped rapidly as I rode him like a boneless rag doll. His back arched, and he groaned loudly. My legs shaking, I collapsed on his chest, clinging to him as he thrust hard and came inside of me. His warm breath stirred my hair, and I listened to the rapid thump of his heart beneath my ear.

"Fuck," he rumbled, "I've never lost control like that."

"Hmm," I said. I was suddenly exhausted. I nuzzled Wes's neck and whimpered in complaint when he eased me off of him.

"Shh, flower girl," he said in a low voice. "Let me get rid of this."

I curled on my side and watched sleepily as he disposed of the condom before pulling the covers from under me. He pulled them up over both of us and spooned me before kissing me on the back of the shoulder.

"Should I leave?"

"Nuh-uh," I said before yawning. "Do you need to call your mom and ask her if you can have a sleepover at a friend's house?"

His laughter made his chest vibrate against my back, and I twitched when he gave me a playful slap on the butt. "Smart ass. Go to sleep, flower girl."

"Yeah, kay," I mumbled. "It was terrific, Wes."

"It really was," he whispered before kissing my shoulder again.

"DAISY, WAKE UP. C'MON, WE GOTTA GO."

I muttered a curse and pushed at the hand that was poking me in the forehead. "Stop it."

"It's time to wake up."

I opened my eyes and stared blearily at Frannie. "What?"

"We have to go," she said as she sat on the other double bed. "I told my mom we were leaving the city early this morning and would be at her place by ten, and it's nine-thirty."

I suddenly sat up, clutching the blankets to my naked chest and staring wild-eyed behind me. The bed was empty, and there was no sign of Wes or his clothing. I breathed a sigh of relief as Frannie gave me a curious look.

"What?"

"Nothing," I said.

"You looked weird for a minute there."

"You look weird."

"Shut up."

"You shut up."

"Hey, Daisy?"

"Yeah?"

"Why are you naked?"

I blinked at Frannie before clearing my throat. "Uh, I was really hot last night. Plus, I always sleep in the nude."

"Sure you do." Frannie collapsed on her back and stared up at the ceiling. "I guess as your girlfriend, I should know that."

"You really should." I sat up, keeping the bed covers wrapped around me, and ran a hand through my hair. "I need a shower."

"Why do you have just-been-fucked hair?" Frannie asked suddenly.

"I don't," I said.

"Yes, you do."

"No, I don't."

"Yes, you do."

"Shut up."

"You shut up."

"Grab my robe out of my suitcase, would you?" I said in exasperation as Frannie grinned at me.

"Listen, honey, I'm all for you getting laid, but try not to forget that you're pretending to be my girlfriend, okay? You can't be fucking random guys all week."

"I won't!" I said. Frannie dug through my suitcase and pulled out my robe. "It was a one-time thing. Besides, it's your fault. You were the one who told me to go to the bar and have a drink."

Frannie laughed and handed me my robe before kissing me on the forehead. "I'll take the blame for it. Honestly, I'm glad you found someone to have a little fun with. We've lived together for nearly six months, and you haven't had sex once. I'm surprised things haven't dried up down there."

I glared at her, and she giggled before kissing my forehead again. "Seriously, though, good for you. Now, get your butt in that shower so we can go to my parents' house and pretend to be lesbians."

Frannie's childhood home was a cute little two-story with grey brick and dark blue trim and shutters. As I pulled into the driveway and shut the car off, Frannie said, "Dad's truck isn't here. I thought Mom said he was finished work already."

We climbed out of the car, and Frannie stared at the house to our right. It was a similar-looking two-story, covered with cream-coloured siding, and the trim and shutters were a cheery red. A large oak tree grew between the houses, and Frannie grinned at me.

"When we were kids, Dad and Owen's dad got into a fight over that tree. It's smack dab in the middle of both our properties, and they almost came to blows over who it actually belonged to."

"Sounds like a fun memory," I said as I grabbed my suitcase from the trunk. Frannie laughed and grabbed her own bag before slamming the trunk lid shut. "That's Owen's bedroom right there. It's right across from mine."

She stared up at the window on the second floor with a look of longing on her face. I nudged her with my elbow. "Hey, try not to be so obvious, would you?"

She sighed. "You're right. I just miss him so much already."

"It's been what? An hour since you saw him?" I said as we headed up the sidewalk toward the front door.

"Yeah, but we only had time for sex once this morning," Frannie said in a low voice.

I rolled my eyes. A mental image of riding Wes flickered through my head, and a shameful amount of liquid immediately dampened the crotch of my panties. I shifted my suitcase to my other hand. I had to admit that I was a little upset he had left without waking me up and saying goodbye, but I had been the one who told him it was only sex last night. Still, waking me up would have been the polite thing to do.

Are you mad that he didn't wake you up to say goodbye, or mad that he didn't wake you up to have sex again?

I ignored my inner voice and followed Frannie as she opened the front door and stepped into the narrow hallway. She dropped her suitcase with a loud thump and shouted, "Mom? We're here!"

A slender, blonde woman stepped into the hallway and made a loud squeal of happiness. "Oh, Frannie!" She hugged Frannie before kissing her on the cheek. "I'm so glad you're home."

"Me too, Mom," Frannie said. We hung up our jackets and took off our boots. Frannie indicated for me to follow them as her mom took her hand and tugged her down the hallway to the kitchen. The kitchen was small and tidy, featuring a little nook at the end. A heavy-set man with an iPad in his hand and an older woman with short white hair were sitting at the table placed in the nook, and Frannie hurried over to hug both of them.

"Hi, Dad. I didn't see your truck out front, so I thought you weren't here."

"Your brother has it," Frannie's mom said as she grabbed mugs from the cupboard. "I asked him to run to Phil's Buy and Save for me."

"It's good to see you Frannie-pants." Her father had a deep voice, and he hugged Frannie before sitting back down. "How was the drive?"

"Fine," Frannie said. "The roads weren't bad. Hi, Grandma."

"Francine, you look so cute today," the older woman said as Frannie bent and kissed her cheek. "You're in love. Who's the lucky boy?"

Frannie jerked all over before giving her grandmother a guilty look. "Grandma, I'm not in love."

"Of course you are," her grandmother said. "I can see it on your face."

Frannie's mom laughed. "Mother Francine, hush now." She turned toward me. "You must be Daisy."

"I am," I said. "It's nice to meet you, Mrs. McKinley."

I held out my hand and squeaked in surprise when Frannie's mother gave me a tight hug.

"Oh, please, call me Patricia or Mom," she said. "We aren't formal around here."

"Uh, sure, okay," I said. Frannie stepped toward me and put her arm around my waist. I tried to look natural as Frannie took a deep breath.

"Mom, Dad, I have something to tell you. Daisy and I aren't just roommates. We're, um, dating."

There was complete silence, and I gripped Frannie's hand when it slid into mine. She cleared her throat and said, "I'm a lesbian."

"You're a what?" Her father said.

"She's a lesbian," Frannie's grandmother said. "It means she likes to have sex with other women, Gregory."

"I know what it means, Mom!" Her father's face turned red.

Frannie clutched my hand in a death grip before staring at her mother. Patricia bit her bottom lip as tears slid down her cheeks.

"Mom, please don't cry," Frannie pleaded. "Don't be upset, okay? I know this is a shock, but - "

"Upset?" her mother said. "Honey, I'm not upset. I'm crying because I'm so happy!"

Frannie gave me a bewildered look as her mother threw her arms around both of us and hugged us hard. "I was so worried that you were all alone in that horrible city, but you aren't! You're in love! Oh, honey. I'm so happy for you both! And honestly, I always suspected that you were a lesbian."

Frannie gaped at her, and I bit the inside of my cheek to stop the laughter from spilling out.

"You suspected that I was a lesbian?"

Patricia nodded. "Of course I did, dear." She kissed both of us on the cheeks and stepped back before wiping the tears away. "Gregory, say something to your daughter."

Frannie's father was already scrolling through his iPad again. He looked up and said, "Happy for you, honey. Hey, did you hear that I'm the head of the historical society of Darville now?"

"Yes, Dad," Frannie said. "We already talked about it."

"Right, right," he said as Frannie's grandmother stood up with a grunt and walked slowly toward us. She took both of our hands and squeezed them.

"I knew you were in love, Francine," she said with a grin. "You can't hide that from your grandma."

"I guess not," Frannie said with a quick look at me.

"Now, Daisy, do you want kids?" her grandmother asked.

"Grandma!" Frannie said. "It's a little soon to be talking kids."

"It isn't." Patricia added coffee in neat little scoops to the filter in the coffee machine. "As lesbians, it won't be as simple to get pregnant. You'll need to decide if you want to do sperm donation or adoption, and if adoption, are you adopting a baby or an older child, and are you adopting locally or internationally. There are lots of decisions to make, not to mention whether you are going to get married here at home or - "

"Mom!" Frannie said. "Stop talking about marriage and kids. You're freaking out Daisy."

"I'm sorry, Daisy," Patricia said with a warm smile. "Sometimes I do get a little enthusiastic about my kids."

"Uh, that's okay," I said.

There was an awkward silence, and Frannie said, "So, we'll just take my suitcase to my room and Daisy's down-stairs to the basement. We'll be right back."

"Downstairs?" Patricia said. "Honey, don't be silly. Daisy can stay in your room with you."

"Oh, um, that's fine," Frannie said. "I told Daisy that we would have to, um, have separate bedrooms, and she's fine with it. Aren't you, Daisy?"

"Yes," I said. "It's not a problem."

"Oh, please," Patricia said. "You act as though everyone in this house is an old fuddy-duddy. We're perfectly fine with you sleeping in the same bed together. But do remember that both your father and I are light sleepers, so if you're going to have sex, keep the - "

"Mom!" Frannie said as her face turned bright red.

Patricia shrugged. "No need to be embarrassed, sweetie. Sex is perfectly natural."

Before Frannie could reply, we heard the front door slam and a deep voice said, "Mom? I'm back."

The blood drained from my face at the sound of the familiar voice, and my entire body stiffened as I tightened my grip on Frannie's hand. She winced and tried to pull her hand away. "Daisy, ouch!"

"I got the lemon pepper, but Phil says they've never heard of tarragon. I'm not shocked. Honestly, I'm surprised they have spices beyond salt and pepper."

I stood frozen to the spot as Wes, my one-night stand with the perfect goddamn body, walked into the kitchen.

CHAPTER 4

Wes

"Hey, Wes," my sister said.

I barely noticed Frannie. All the breath had been sucked from my body, and I stared dumbfounded at Daisy. What the fuck was she doing standing in my mother's kitchen? And why the fuck was she holding my sister's hand?

Before I could say anything, Daisy dropped Frannie's hand and stepped toward me. She held her hand out and said, "Hi, I'm Daisy! You must be Frannie's brother. I'm Daisy! It's nice to meet you! I'm Frannie's, um, roommate."

I stared at her hand for a moment before shifting the bag of groceries to my left. I took her hand and was immediately thrust into the memory of Daisy riding me, of her nails digging into my wrist – hell, I still had the marks from her nails on my chest and wrist – and the way her perfect tits had tasted.

"Don't be so shy, Daisy," my mother said. "Wes isn't a prude. Daisy is Frannie's girlfriend, honey."

My hand squeezed Daisy's compulsively. Girlfriend? Daisy was Frannie's girlfriend? I decided I had misheard my mother.

"Girlfriend," I said in a weird voice that didn't sound at all like my normal one. "Meaning, you're her friend and you're a girl."

"No, dearest," my grandmother said from her spot at the table. "It means that Daisy is Frannie's lesbian lover. They're having sex."

"Grandma!" Frannie said as my mouth dropped open. Daisy yanked her hand free of mine as Frannie joined us and slipped her arm around Daisy's waist. She hesitated and then pressed a brief kiss against Daisy's mouth.

Hot and unpleasant jealousy immediately tingled down my spine. I placed the groceries on the floor and took a step back. What the fuck was going on?

"Wes, are you okay?" Frannie said. "You look kind of pale."

"I'm fine," I said hoarsely. I stared at Daisy. She was as pale as I was, and she gave me a worried look before glancing at Frannie and then shaking her head very slightly. It was more than evident that she wanted me to keep my mouth shut.

"How long have you been dating?" I asked.

"Uh, only a few months," Frannie said.

I stared at Daisy, who wore a bright look of desperation. After a moment, I said, "Nice to meet you."

Relief flooded her face. "It's nice to meet you, too."

I bent and picked up the grocery bags as Frannie grabbed Daisy's hand. "We'll grab our suitcases and put them in my room. Be right back."

She dragged Daisy out of the room, and I set the grocery bags on the counter. "Since when did Frannie become a lesbian?"

"Oh, I always suspected," my mother said as she emptied the bags. "I'm happy for her. Very happy. You know, it doesn't matter to me or your father who you date." She gave me a meaningful look. "We'll love you no matter your life choices."

"I'm not gay, Mom," I said.

"I know, honey." She pinched my cheek affectionately. "I just want you to know that we love you no matter what. Unless you never get married and give me grandchildren. That will get you kicked out of the will. Okay?"

She smiled sweetly at me, and I nodded. "Yep, got it."

"Good. Now, you still haven't told me where you were last night."

I cleared my throat. Somehow, telling my mother that I was screwing my sister's lying, cheating girlfriend didn't seem like a smart thing to say. As anger burned in my belly, I said, "I caught up with some old friends and ended up crashing on their couch."

"Isn't that lovely," my mother said.

"Yeah. I'm going to go have a shower." I kissed my mother's cheek and left the kitchen, climbing the steps two at a time. I paused in front of my sister's room and raised my hand to knock before changing my mind. My shock at seeing Daisy had turned to anger. She had seemed sweet last night, and the sex had been the best of my life, but any lingering affection for her or regret I'd felt this morning from leaving without saying goodbye had disappeared. She was lying and cheating on my baby sister. I would find out what kind of game she was playing and then give her the choice to tell my sister what she had done, or I would.

Daisy

43

I SLIPPED OUTSIDE INTO THE COLD NIGHT AIR AND TOOK A FEW deep breaths. It was almost nine, and I had a headache and felt nearly sick to my stomach from the tension between Wes and me. Not that Frannie or the rest of her family had seemed to notice. We had gone shopping with Patricia and Frannie's grandmother for a few hours in the afternoon before returning to the house. I had tried to avoid Wes as best I could, but the house was small and every time I turned around, he was there. Staring at me with those dark eyes. They were cold and angry without a single hint of the warmth that was there last night. I shivered delicately and zipped up my jacket before walking around to the side of the house and leaning against the cold brick.

I had told Frannie I needed to grab something from my car, but what I really needed was a moment to myself. Or, more accurately, a moment away from Wes and his barely contained rage with me. Fuck, I had really screwed things up. What were the odds that my one-night stand would be with Frannie's brother?

I rubbed at my temples and tried to think past the headache. Okay, I could fix this. I needed to get Wes alone and give him a condensed version of the truth. He didn't need to know that Frannie was dating Owen. I would tell him that Frannie was trying to avoid being set up and that –

"Thinking of escaping into the night?"

I made a breathless squeal and jerked against the brick before staring wide-eyed at Wes. "Oh my God, you scared me! Don't sneak up on a person like that."

"Sorry."

"No, you're not," I said.

"No, I'm really not," he said in a voice that was colder than the brick I was leaning against.

"Wes, listen, I know you're wondering what's going on and I – oh, God!"

Moving quickly, Wes stepped in front of me and rested his hands on the wall on either side of my head. His body brushed up against mine, and even through our jackets, my body remembered the heat of his. I was shamefully aroused instantly. My hips pressed instinctively against him, and I blushed when he jerked his pelvis away from mine and said, "Are you fucking kidding me, right now?"

"I'm sorry," I said. "I can explain."

"Can you?" he growled. "He lowered his face until it was only inches from mine. "That's good, because I'd really like an explanation for why last night I was balls deep in a woman who turns out to be my baby sister's lesbian lover."

"I'm not a lesbian," I said quickly.

"No? So, you're a cheating bisexual instead of a cheating lesbian?"

"I'm not a cheater or bisexual or - "

"What kind of game are you playing? Is your name even Daisy?"

"What? Of course it is! Wes, I know you're angry, but listen for - "

"Does my sister know that you're a damn cheater?"

"Shut up!" I suddenly snapped at him.

He blinked in surprise at my sudden burst of anger as I glared up at him. "Shut your big, stupid mouth and let me explain before you make a complete ass of yourself."

"Fine. Explain yourself."

I took a deep breath and said, "I'm your sister's room-mate. Frannie has been dating a man for the last year that she doesn't think your family will approve of. She knows your mom and grandmother were going to try to set her up with someone during the Christmas holidays, so she begged me to pretend to be her lesbian lover so that they would leave her alone. Against my better judgment, I agreed. I'm not a lesbian or bisexual. I am playing a part for your sister because she's very important to me and I love her. Like a sister."

I took another deep breath and stared up at Wes. He wouldn't believe me. Why would he? It was a crazy, stupid story.

"Who's the guy?"

"I'm sorry?" I stared at him in shock.

"Who's the guy she's dating?" he asked.

"I don't know," I lied.

He studied me closely before pressing his body against mine. This time, he didn't move away when my pelvis pushed against his. "You're a terrible liar, flower girl."

I bit my bottom lip as my gaze flickered to Owen's bedroom window. "I don't know."

"So, you're telling me that you're roommates with my sister and have never once seen or met the guy she's dating?" He breathed into my ear.

"Y-yes," I said unsteadily.

He stepped back and raised his eyebrows. "Tell me, Daisy."

My eyes flickered to Owen's bedroom window again, and I cursed inwardly when Wes followed my gaze.

"Owen?" he asked. "Frannie is dating Owen Brenner?"

"You can't say anything," I said frantically. "You can't tell your parents. Frannie will kill me if you do."

He rubbed his big hand through his hair before glancing at Owen's bedroom again. "What the hell does she see in that guy?"

"He's a good guy," I said.

"Doesn't he work at a Best Buy?"

"He's a manager there," I said defensively. "Listen, I know you have this family feud thing going on, but you can't say anything, okay?"

He stared blankly at me. "Say anything? Are you kidding

me? I'll take this goddamn secret to my grave. If Dad finds out that Frannie is dating Owen Brenner, he'll have a fucking heart attack."

He rubbed at his own temples before shaking his head. "Fucking hell. What is Frannie thinking?"

"She loves him," I said. "She loves him and they're good together. He's a great guy and he treats her really well."

Wes didn't reply, and I gave him a few seconds before I said, "So, uh, what do we do about the other thing?"

"What other thing?"

"What do you mean 'what other thing'?" I said. "I slept with my best friend/fake lesbian lover's brother!"

Wes shrugged. "You didn't know who I was."

"Damn straight I didn't!" I glared at him. "That's entirely your fault, by the way."

He gave me a look of confusion. "What?"

"I'm friends with Frannie on Facebook, Instagram, and Twitter. I know all of her friends and family on there, but I have never once seen you on her friend feed or even a picture of you!"

He shrugged. "I'm not on social media and I hate having my picture taken."

"Not on social media? Who the hell isn't on social media?" I sputtered.

"You can't tell me my sister has never mentioned me by name," Wes said.

"I – I – maybe she did," I stammered. "I really don't remember. But if she had, there's more than one Wes in the world."

He grinned, and I scowled at him. "If you had a goddamn Facebook account, none of this would have happened. I would have known exactly who you were the minute you waltzed up to me at that bar and started flirting with me. It would have been a hard no, buddy!"

"Flirting with you? I think what you're trying to say is when I came up and saved your cute ass from that drunk guy," Wes said.

"I had it all under control," I said. "Until you came along with your perfect body and your perfect mouth and your... giant perfect dick!"

Wes burst into laughter, and after a moment, I started to giggle too. I buried my face in my hands and said, "I'm sorry. I don't really think it's your fault."

"Nothing has changed," Wes said. "We were two people who agreed to have one fun night together. It's a little awkward now, but we're both adults. We can handle a little awkwardness for a week, right?"

"Yeah," I said as I dropped my hands. They were turning ice cold, I was shivering madly, and I could barely feel the tip of my nose. I needed to go back inside, but instead I said, "You didn't say goodbye this morning."

"I should have."

"Why didn't you?" I asked. When he didn't reply, I said, "Was it because I wasn't that great in bed?"

He immediately shook his head, and I couldn't stop my low moan when he put his arm around my waist and drew me into his embrace. He kissed the tip of my cold nose and said, "I didn't wake you up because I didn't have another condom."

"What?" I asked in confusion, ignoring my instinct to burrow against his warm body.

"I didn't have another condom," he repeated patiently, "and if I had woken you up to say goodbye, I would have kissed you. If I had kissed you, then I would have touched you. If I had touched you, then I would have fucked you."

I blushed bright red and stared at the snow on the ground. "Oh."

He pulled me closer and nuzzled my neck. "I had an

48

amazing time last night, Daisy. I know you have a vow of celibacy going on, but I want to make you break that vow repeatedly."

I shivered all over, this time from need instead of cold, before pulling away. "I can't, Wes. I'm pretending to be your sister's girlfriend, remember?"

He sighed and nodded. "Yeah, I remember."

"We'd better go back inside."

"You go first," he said.

"You won't say anything about Owen, will you?" I said.

He shook his head. "No, I won't."

Wes

"MOM, WE'LL BE FINE. WE HAVE SNOW IN THE CITY." Frannie's voice held a note of impatience. "Besides, we're only going to the mall, and it's like a twenty-minute drive."

I wandered into the kitchen, my gaze automatically dropping to Daisy's ass. She was bent over the dishwasher, putting her plate in the bottom rack, and I could feel my dick twitching. I quickly looked away from her ass. Jesus, I needed to get some control.

"I don't know why you have to go today," Mom said. "It's snowing like crazy, and the roads will be slippery."

"We'll be fine," Frannie said as Daisy straightened and turned around. She gave me a tentative smile as Frannie grabbed her jacket from the back of the chair. "Daisy has a waxing appointment."

This time, my gaze dropped to Daisy's crotch before I could stop it. She cleared her throat, and I forced myself to look at her. She was blushing brightly, and I really wanted to grin at her. I found it strange that she had made the waxing appointment. Last night, she had made it clear that we couldn't have sex again. So, why the sudden waxing appointment?

I wondered if I could convince her not to wax her sweet little pussy. It was her body and none of my business what she did with it, but I wasn't lying when I told her I preferred the natural look. I scowled inwardly at the thought of her soft curls being ripped out with hot wax before I reminded myself that it didn't matter anyway. I wouldn't be seeing her pussy again, whether it was natural or waxed bare.

"Why don't you let Wes drive you in Dad's truck?" Mom said. "Honey, do you mind? I would feel so much better about the girls' being out in this weather if you drove them."

I took a quick look at Frannie. She shook her head and gave me a pointed look. I grinned at her and said, "Sure, I don't mind at all."

"No," Frannie said with another pointed look at me. "Daisy is perfectly happy to drive in this weather, and we don't need my big brother tagging along with us. Isn't that right, Daisy?"

Daisy hesitated, and Frannie elbowed her in the side. "Isn't that right?"

"Um, yes. I'm fine with driving." She chewed on her bottom lip, and despite having just met her, I knew she was lying.

"I'll drive," I said as Frannie gave me a death glare and Daisy gave me a look of gratitude.

"You can't hang out with us," Frannie snapped. "We have," she hesitated, "girl stuff to do."

"Yeah, yeah," I said. "I'll do my own thing, and you can text me when you're ready to go home."

"Perfect!" Mom said. "I feel so much better about this plan."

She followed us out of the kitchen and into the hallway,

chatting happily as we pulled on our boots and our coats. "Daisy, honey, you don't have a scarf."

"I forgot it," Daisy said.

"I'll crochet you one tonight," Mom said. "You'll need one for when we get the Christmas tree."

"You don't have to do that, Patricia," Daisy protested. I grinned to myself. Daisy didn't know it yet, but she was fighting a losing battle.

"Of course I do! You're part of our family now, sweetheart," Mom said. "What's your favourite colour?"

"Oh, uh, I like red," Daisy said.

"Fantastic! I picked up the softest red yarn the other day!" Mom said. "It'll make a perfect scarf for you. Now," she kissed Frannie's cheek, then Daisy's, and finally mine, "be careful out there, you three, and be home for dinner, please."

"Yes, Mom," Frannie said as she glanced at her cell phone. "Wes, let's go for God's sake. I don't want to be late for..."

She gave Daisy a sudden blank look.

"My appointment," Daisy said quickly.

"Right. Her appointment." Frannie took Daisy's hand and dragged her out of the house.

I followed them to the truck. The snow was falling heavily, and I studied the flakes that were caught in Daisy's eyelashes as Frannie opened the passenger door. "Daisy, get in."

"What? No, I want the outside," Daisy said with a nervous look at me.

"No way," Frannie said. "I hate sitting in the middle. Get in, Daisy."

She sighed. "Fine."

Dad's truck was old, loud, and had a bench seat. The thought of Daisy sitting next to me made me nearly as giddy as a goddamn schoolgirl. As I watched her struggle to climb into the truck, I brushed past Frannie and put my hands around Daisy's waist. She made an adorable little squeak as I lifted her into the truck.

"Uh, thank you, Wes," she said.

"No problem." I boosted Frannie into the truck and slammed the passenger door shut before crossing to the driver's side. I leaned in, started the truck, and grabbed the snow brush before turning the heat on high and closing the door. I cleared off the windshield and hood of snow, then climbed into the truck.

"Ready?" I asked.

Daisy nodded. Frannie was texting on her phone, and she made an impatient gesture with her hand. "God, yes. Drive on, Jeeves."

I rolled my eyes and pulled out of the driveway and onto the street. Daisy's leg was pressed against mine, and it was taking all of my willpower not to put my hand on her thigh. She was wearing yoga pants, and they clung to her firm thighs. Christ, yoga pants had never turned me on so much before. I ignored my hardening dick and concentrated on driving. The roads weren't actually that great, making for slow going. By the time we reached the mall parking lot, Frannie was nearly shaking with impatience.

"Finally!" she muttered as I parked and shut off the truck. Her phone rang and she glanced at it, a happy little smile crossing her face. "This is a private call. Give me a minute."

She opened the door and slid out of the truck, slamming the door behind her. She wandered away, speaking into her phone as I turned to Daisy. "That was Owen, wasn't it?"

Daisy nodded. "Yeah, that was his ring. She's meeting him here for a few hours."

"Do you have a waxing appointment?" I asked.

"Yes." She blushed brightly and stared at the back of Frannie's head. "Thank you for driving us. It makes me a little anxious to drive in bad weather."

"You're welcome." I glanced around the parking lot. There was no one walking by, and Frannie wasn't looking at us.

I placed my hand on Daisy's thigh, rubbing it firmly as she gave me a startled look. "Wh-what are you doing?"

"What are you getting waxed?" I slipped my fingers between her legs and rubbed her inner thigh.

Her soft little moan made my dick harden. I pulled on her thigh, pleased when she immediately widened her legs. I let my hand inch up a little higher. "What are you getting waxed, flower girl?"

"You know what," she whispered. "Wes, your sister is right there."

"She's not looking," I said. "Are you sure you want to wax your sweet little pussy?"

"I... I should."

"I don't think you should." I cupped her pussy through her pants. "I like it just the way it is."

She moaned again. Her cheeks were bright red, and she was biting compulsively at her bottom lip, but she widened her thighs even more. "I usually wax it."

"That's too bad," I said. "But if you insist on waxing, then you need to let me touch those soft little curls of yours one last time."

"What? No, we can't," she said as I pressed rhythmically against her pussy. "Your sister is right there, and we're in the middle of the mall parking lot."

"There's no one around, and Frannie's busy with Owen. Lift your jacket for me, darlin'."

I continued to stare out the windshield, watching for others as Daisy hesitated. "Wes, I shouldn't."

"Yes, you should," I said. "Do it, Daisy. I want to touch your pussy."

She moaned and lifted the bottom of her jacket to reveal the waistband of her pants. Moving quickly, I slipped my hand inside her pants and panties and cupped her pussy. She gasped, her thighs clenching around my hand. "Your hand is cold!"

I grinned and stroked her pussy lips. She was wet already, and my dick pressed painfully against my jeans. "You're so warm, darlin'. Warm and wet just for me, isn't that right?"

"Yes," she whispered as she undulated against my hand. She latched onto my arm, staring desperately out the windshield as I rubbed her clit until it swelled against my fingers. I slid my fingers down her slit and pushed one into her tight entrance. She squealed and then clapped her hand over her mouth before lowering it back to my arm.

"Oh God, Wes!"

I moved my hand again, tugging on her soft curls before stroking her clit. She moaned and then said, "Harder."

I didn't reply, and she blushed, giving me a quick look. "Sorry."

"Don't be sorry. Tell me what you want. What you need." I rubbed her clit with rougher strokes.

"Oh, oh God," she whispered. "Smaller circles and a little more pressure and…oh, yes, like that."

She was panting now, her hips rising and falling as bright colour infused her cheeks. Fuck, she was so beautiful, it made me ache. I rubbed hard and fast in small, tight circles against her clit and smiled with satisfaction when she stiffened against my hand and made a low, drawn-out moan. Fresh wetness flooded my fingers as she collapsed against the back of the seat and stared wide-eyed at me.

"Holy crap," she said.

I laughed and she blushed again. "I… that's never happened before."

I gave her a curious look. "What's never happened before?"

"I've never – oh!"

I had suddenly yanked my hand out of her pants and shoved it into my jacket pocket. Frannie was back and reaching for the door. As she opened it, Daisy pulled her jacket down over her crotch and gave Frannie a bright smile.

"Hi!"

"Hey." Frannie frowned at her. "What's wrong?"

"Nothing's wrong," Daisy said.

"Do you feel okay? Your face is really red."

"I feel fine. Ready to go?"

"Yes," Frannie gave her a doubtful look. "You sure you're okay?"

"Of course." Daisy slid across the seat and out of the truck. I stayed where I was, praying like hell that Frannie didn't notice the prominent bulge at the front of my pants.

Frannie turned toward me. "Are you going into the mall?"

I shrugged. "Not sure, Frannie-pants."

"Don't call me that, Wesley," she said with a slight grin. "Thanks for the ride, big brother. I'll text you when we're finished, okay?"

"Yep. Bye, Frannie, bye, Daisy."

"Bye, Wes," Daisy said.

CHAPTER 5

Daisy

I wiped the steam from the bathroom mirror and smoothed my wet hair back from my face. Today had been another stressful day of pretending to be in love with Frannie while trying not to think about how ridiculously attracted I was to Wes. Of course, letting him finger me to an orgasm in the truck this morning probably didn't help me ignore my attraction to him.

I sighed and quickly threw on my pajamas before hanging my towel on the rack. I decided it was much harder to be a pretend lesbian when you wanted to hump the leg of your pretend girlfriend's brother every time you got within ten feet of him. I smoothed cream onto my freshly-waxed legs and combed my hair before gathering my toiletry bag and dirty clothes.

It was just after eleven and I was ready for bed. Frannie's dad had made the entire family play Monopoly with him after dinner, and the damn game had gone on for nearly four hours. Wes and Frannie had engaged in sibling trash talking that made me laugh before Wes kicked all of our butts and won the game. I had to admit that I found his competitive spirit a teeny bit attractive.

I opened the bathroom door and stepped out into the hallway. Hopefully, I would sleep and not lie awake and think about Wes naked and –

"I like your pajamas."

I jumped about a foot and squinted at Wes in the dim hallway. He was leaning against the wall with his arms crossed over his broad chest, and - oh sweet Jesus have mercy - he was wearing only a pair of sleep pants that were barely hanging onto his hips.

I swallowed hard and clutched my toiletry bag and clothes against my braless chest with one hand as I tugged self-consciously at my shorts with the other. "What are you doing here?"

"Waiting to use the washroom?" He arched his eyebrow at me, and I cleared my throat.

"Right, of course. Sorry, I took so long."

"That's fine," he said.

He stayed where he was, and my nipples hardened when he gave my body a slow, hungry look.

"Wes," I whispered, "don't look at me like that."

"Like what, little flower?" He said in his low and raspy voice.

"You know like what," I said shakily. "I… goodnight, Wes."

"Good night, Daisy."

I slipped by him, making sure to leave lots of room between our bodies and stepped inside Frannie's bedroom. "I am so ready for bed, Fran – oh my God, Frannie!"

Owen and Frannie sat up on the bed as I glared at them. "What the hell!"

"Keep your voice down," Frannie whispered.

"What are you doing here, Owen?" I said in a low voice.

"Dude, I miss my lady," Owen said.

"You saw her this morning."

"Yeah, but I couldn't, like, touch her or anything."

I rolled my eyes. "Are you being serious right now? How did you even get in here?"

He grinned at me and pointed to the window. "I totally used the tree to go from my bedroom to my lady's bedroom."

Frannie giggled and kissed his cheek. "You're so smart, baby."

"Well, sorry to break up your little love nest, but I'm tired and I want to go to sleep," I said.

"Daisy," Frannie gave me a look that would melt butter, "we really miss each other. I need a little time with my baby."

"What my lady is trying to say is we want to bone," Owen said cheerfully.

"No!" I said. "No way, Frannie. I am not staying in here while you two bang like bunnies. That's disgusting."

"You don't have to stay," Frannie said.

"But I'm cool with it if you do," Owen said.

I glared at him as Frannie smacked him on the chest. "Behave, baby."

"Go to his room!" I said in a fierce whisper.

"I can't climb across that tree," Frannie said. "Besides, we have the extra room in the basement, remember? Mom and Dad usually get up at seven. As long as you come back upstairs to my room before seven, they'll never know you slept down there."

"Frannie, no. You guys can wait until we get back home."

"Dude, no," Owen said. "I can't. I've already got a wicked case of blue balls."

"Ugh," I said.

"Please, Oopsie-Daisy," Frannie said. "It's really stressful for me being around my family. I need to relieve it somehow!"

"Have you thought about a long, hot shower?" I snapped.

"It's not my fault," Frannie said. "I didn't think my mom would be cool with us sharing a room, you know?"

"Frannie..."

She gave me another pleading look. "Please, honey."

"Fine! But if you get caught screwing Owen, I'll play the jilted lover card with your family. Do you understand?"

"I do. We won't get caught," Frannie said happily. "Thank you so much, Daisy. You're the best."

"Yeah," I muttered as I dropped my clothes and toiletry bag into my suitcase. "Good night."

"Good night." Frannie was already lying back on the bed next to Owen, and I slipped out of the room quickly, forcing myself not to slam the door.

I groaned inwardly. Wes was heading into his bedroom, and he gave me a curious look. "What's wrong?"

"Nothing," I said.

"Tell the truth, please."

I sighed and crossed my arms over my chest before whispering, "Turns out that Owen is like a damn monkey and crawled across the tree to your sister's room, because they can't go more than forty-eight hours without having sex. Now I'm banished to the basement so your sister can get lucky."

"Gross," Wes said.

"Yeah. Anyway, good night."

"The bed in the basement is really uncomfortable. Mine is much more comfortable."

"That's sweet of you to offer to give up your bed," I said tartly, "but I've slept in uncomfortable beds before."

He grinned at me as I pushed past him and started toward the staircase. "Hey, Daisy?"

"Yeah?"

"My parents are really light sleepers. What excuse are you going to give them for sleeping in the basement?"

"I'll be quiet. They'll never know."

"They'll hear you. See that floorboard with the knot in it? The minute you cross over it, my mom will wake up and she'll be out of her bedroom to find out what's wrong."

"You're only saying that to try and get me into your bed."

"Nope, I'm telling you what I've learned from years of trying to sneak out of the house as a teenager. You're going to get caught."

"I'm better at sneaking out than you."

He grinned. "Good luck then, flower girl."

I stuck my tongue out at him, and his grin widened before he ducked into his bedroom and shut the door.

I took a deep breath and crept down the hallway. I stepped over the floorboard that Wes had pointed out and paused, holding my breath and listening intently. There was nothing, and I snorted to myself before moving to the top of the staircase. Wes was full of crap, just like I knew –

"Daisy? Sweetheart, what's wrong?"

I groaned inwardly and turned to smile at Patricia. "Nothing."

A door further down opened, and Frannie's grandmother stuck her head out. "What's going on?"

"There's something wrong with Daisy," Patricia said.

She hurried out of her room as Gregory hollered from inside their room, "What's wrong with Daisy?"

"There's nothing wrong," I said quickly. "I was getting a drink of water."

"Oh, sweetie, I have bottles of water right here in this closet." Patricia opened the linen closet door.

"What's wrong?" Gregory hollered again.

"She's thirsty!" Frannie's grandmother shouted back.

"Get her some water from the closet!" Gregory yelled.

"I am, love," Patricia said.

She pulled out a bottle of water and handed it to me. "Here, sweetheart."

"Thank you," I said.

"Oh, don't mention it," she said as Frannie's grandma retreated into her room and closed the door. "I started leaving bottles of water in the closet when Wes and Francine were teenagers. They were constantly getting up in the night and going downstairs for water. I figured it would be easier to keep bottles of water up here, and just never lost the habit after they moved out."

She leaned forward and kissed my cheek before stroking my damp hair. "You're such a lovely girl, Daisy. We're so glad you're dating our Frannie."

Guilt trickled through me, and I clutched the water bottle before giving her a weak smile. "Thank you, Patricia. I really like your family."

"We like you too, sweetheart. Now, hurry back to Frannie. I'm sure she misses you."

"Goodnight, Patricia."

"Goodnight, Daisy."

I headed back toward Frannie's bedroom, pausing with my hand on the doorknob. Thankfully, Patricia had already returned to her bedroom and shut the door. I leaned against the door, but when I heard Owen make a low moan, I straightened and hurried away toward Wes's room.

I stared at his door for a moment before cursing under my breath and opening it. I slipped into his room and shut the door behind me. His room was on the smaller side, and the twin bed was tucked against the far wall under the window. Moonlight spilled across his bed, and I stared at his big body lying in the bed as he sat up on his elbows.

"Went with the old 'I'm getting a drink of water' excuse, huh? Rookie mistake."

"How was I supposed to know your mother kept bottles of water in the linen closet?" I said. "No one does that. You could have warned me."

"I could have, but where's the fun in that?"

I avoided looking at his naked chest as I crossed the room and set the water down on his nightstand. "Move over."

"Nope, I sleep on the outside, flower girl."

"I hate sleeping on the inside," I huffed. "It's too crowded and…oh God."

Wes had pulled back the covers, and I stared at his big, naked body and tried not to drool.

"Y-you're naked," I stuttered.

"I always sleep naked," he said with a wicked grin. "Don't you?"

His gaze dropped to my breasts, and I could feel my nipples hardening in response. His grin widened, and I crossed my arms over my chest as his cock turned fully erect.

"Behave." I carefully crawled over his shins and lay on the bed next to him. It was crowded, Wes was a big man, and the bed was on the small side. I shifted to my side to face him as he tucked his hands under his head and stared at the ceiling. The way his dick was tenting the sheets didn't seem to embarrass him at all.

"Nice room," I said. "So, did you have a crush on Anne Hathaway as a teenager?"

"How can you tell?" He laughed.

"Maybe it's the hundreds of Anne Hathaway posters plastered on your walls?"

He laughed again. "She's hot. What teenage boy didn't have a crush on her?"

I sat up a little and squinted in the darkness at the shelf on the far wall. "What are all those trophies for?"

"Football."

"Do you find it weird to come back home and have everything the same in your bedroom?" I asked.

"No, not really. Mom has said more than once that she's turning my room into a craft room and Frannie's room into an exercise room, but it hasn't happened yet.

I settled onto my side again and stared at his profile in the moonlight. God, he was handsome. "Your family is great."

"They are," he said. "My mom can be a bit overbearing sometimes, but it comes from a good place."

"I don't mind. It's kind of nice to have someone 'mothering' me again."

"I'm really sorry for your loss."

"Thank you. So, where did you learn to be so merciless at Monopoly?"

He laughed. "My grandpa. He was ruthless at board games. Even when we were kids, he showed no mercy. I don't think I ever beat him at checkers. Once I was complaining to my mom about the fact that grandpa never let me win, and he came thumping into the kitchen and said, 'Son, it don't mean nothin' if I let you win. Now stop your whining and come help me mow the lawn.'"

"I think I would have liked your grandpa," I said.

"He would have really liked you," Wes said. "In fact, my entire family seems to really like you. They're going to be awfully disappointed when you and Frannie break up."

I didn't say anything. I could feel the heat of his body, and it was taking everything in me not to curl up against him.

"How did your waxing appointment go?" he suddenly asked.

"Fine." I couldn't resist rubbing my leg against his. "Nice and smooth now."

He groaned and shifted to his side to face me before cupping my face and stroking his thumb across my mouth.

"Wes," I said unsteadily as he shifted closer until his body was touching mine. "This is a bad idea."

"I like bad ideas," he whispered before kissing me.

I returned his kiss immediately, throwing my arm around him and rubbing his broad back as he cupped my thigh and draped it over his hip before stroking my leg.

"Better?" I asked.

"Very smooth," he said, "but I like the Sasquatch version of Daisy too."

I smacked him on the back, and he laughed before pressing his cock against me. We were separated only by the thin material of my pajama shorts, and I made another soft moan when he cupped my breast.

"Daisy," now his voice was unsteady, "if you don't want me to fuck you, tell me now so I can get out of the damn bed and sleep on the floor."

"You don't have to sleep on the floor," I whispered.

"Thank fucking God," he muttered before kissing me hard. I sucked on his tongue, and he groaned, then rolled me onto my back and pressed one thigh between mine. I rubbed against him as he lifted his upper body, and I helped him pull my shirt off.

"I've missed your beautiful tits," he said in a low voice before dipping his head and capturing one hard nipple in his mouth. He sucked with firm pressure, and I moaned in pleasure as I clutched at his head.

After only a moment or two, he raised his head and kissed my collarbone. "Daisy?"

"Yeah?"

"What did you mean in the truck when you said that had never happened before?"

Feeling a little stupid, I said, "I always have to touch myself or, you know, help the guy touch me, to have an orgasm. That's the first time I didn't have to."

He gave me a self-satisfied smile. "So, points for Gryffindor then?"

"Like hell you're Gryffindor. You have Hufflepuff written all over you."

He nuzzled my neck, and I stroked the muscles in his back as he licked a slow path up my throat to my ear. "I liked making you come," he whispered.

"I liked it too," I said.

"I really want to taste your pussy."

I shivered all over and couldn't help rubbing my pussy against his thigh.

"Do you want that?"

"Yes, please," I said.

He grinned at me. "Can you be quiet while I'm eating your pussy? The walls are thin."

"Yes," I said.

"If you're too loud, I'll stop," he warned.

"I'll be quiet," I said, even though I didn't know if that was true or not.

He brushed his mouth across mine before tracing my stomach with his fingers. I shivered and twitched and tried not to plead as he made small circles over each of my hipbones. When his hand finally dipped under the waistband of my shorts, my legs were already spread shamefully wide. He touched my pussy, and I giggled at the look of surprise on his face.

The surprise turned to delight as he touched the soft curls. "You didn't wax."

"I couldn't," I said. I tried to sound disapproving. "It's not like I could let someone near my personal bits after you made me come all over your hand ten minutes earlier."

"If I told you that was my brilliant plan all along, would you believe me?" he asked.

"Nope."

"Fair enough. I just wanted to touch you again. I can't seem to get enough of you, flower girl." Wes touched my curls again before moving his hand to the waistband of my shorts. "Let's get these off."

"Yes, let's." I helped him drag my shorts down my legs, and he tossed them on the floor before scooting down the bed and settling his big body between my legs. His shoulders pushed against my thighs, and I ran my fingers through his thick hair as he smiled up at me.

"Remember to be quiet, darlin'."

"I will," I whispered.

His warm, firm lips pressed against my pussy, and I bit back my instant moan of pleasure. He licked down my slit, and I gasped and arched immediately. His hot tongue probed against my entrance, then slipped inside. I moaned loudly, and he stopped and lifted his head.

"Daisy," he warned in a low voice. "Quiet."

"Don't stop," I whispered.

"I haven't even touched your clit and you're already being too loud," he said. "Maybe this isn't a good idea, little flower."

"No, it's a good idea," I whispered frantically. "It's a *great* idea. I'll be quiet."

"Will you?"

"Yes!" I tried to push his face back into my pussy. "Wes, please."

He buried his face between my legs again, and when his tongue swept across my swollen clit, I turned my head and shoved my face into his pillow. Wes flicked his tongue across my clit, licked away the moisture from my swollen lips and then licked my clit with broad, flat sweeps before sucking on my lips. I bucked against his mouth and pressed my face deeper into his pillow. Holy fuck, Wes was a champion pussy eater.

His tongue slicked back and forth over that throbbing

bundle of nerves, and I moaned into the pillow and pumped my pelvis shamelessly against his face. I almost screamed when he rubbed my clit roughly with his thumb and then licked it again. He alternated between the rough strokes with his thumb and the soft, wet licks of his tongue until I lifted my face from the pillow, sucked in a much-needed breath of air and pleaded mindlessly.

"Shh, little flower," he said before delving back into my pussy.

After only touching me twice before, Wes had already learned what I needed to make me come. Pretty fucking impressive considering Richard hadn't figured it out in two goddamn years.

Wes pinched my clit, and I made a muffled scream into the pillow. I was so close, just one rougher pinch would push me into sweet release. Instead of pinching me again, he gave my clit a hard nip. I shrieked into the pillow and climaxed with a dizzying mix of pleasure and pain. Vaguely, I was aware of Wes licking my clit to soothe away the sting before sitting up and reaching into the nightstand drawer for a condom. My body shook as I slowly came down from the high of my orgasm. My stomach muscles were jumping and trembling like live wires, and little aftershocks of pleasure still tingled in my pussy. When Wes pulled the pillow away from my face, I stared blearily up at him. He was already kneeling between my legs, and I widened them automatically as he leaned down and pressed a kiss against my mouth.

"Okay, little flower?"

"So okay," I breathed as I reached between us. My fingers stroked his cock, and he groaned as I helped guide him in.

"Shh," I said. "Thin walls, remember?"

"Fuck, I remember," he muttered as he sheathed himself deep inside my pussy.

I moaned, and he propped himself up on his hands before

staring at my breasts. I pulled on my hard nipples, and he groaned and made two hard thrusts. I gasped and arched up against him before wrapping my legs around his waist.

"So good," he moaned before thrusting in a hard and rough rhythm that made my toes curl. I met each of his strokes, squeezing around his cock with every pump of his hips. He was panting, and his moans were growing progressively louder. I clapped my hand over his mouth as he moved harder and faster. He drove deep one final time and shuddered all over as he climaxed. I could feel the vibration of his low moans against my hand, and I pressed soft kisses on his throat as he shook and thrust back and forth. I moved my hand from his mouth, and he grinned at me before kissing me.

"I really like fucking you, Daisy."

"I really like fucking you, Wes."

He nuzzled my neck affectionately before moving off of me. I turned on my side and watched as he removed the condom and tied it off before tossing it into the trash can near his bed.

"You need to remember to empty the trash can in the morning," I said. "If your mother was cleaning and found that she'd…"

"What? Ground me?" Wes said as he eased back into the bed next to me. He rested on his back, and I curled against his side, running my hand over the hair on his chest as he rubbed lazy circles across my back with his warm hand.

"She'll be suspicious," I said.

"Yep, but not suspicious that it was my sister's girlfriend," Wes said with a low laugh. "Mostly, she'll drive herself crazy trying to figure out how I snuck a girl past her."

"Your mother has crazy good hearing," I said. "Were you ever able to sneak out when you were younger?"

"Once," Wes said.

"Impressive."

"Not really. I was supposed to be sneaking out to meet my friends at the quarry. I made it out of the house but not to the quarry."

"Why not?" I asked.

"I had the brilliant idea to tie my sheets together and climb out the window. Unfortunately, I never did get my 'knots tying' badge from the Boy Scouts."

"Uh oh," I said with a giggle.

"Yeah. The knot came undone at the top, and I fell like a rock."

"Holy shit!"

"Luckily, Dad had planted some rose bushes along the side of the house. They broke my fall, but I still fractured my ankle and got all scratched up from the thorns. I crawled out of the bushes and had to drag my sorry ass to the front door and ring the doorbell."

"You should have gone out Frannie's window and used the tree," I said.

Wes laughed. "Frannie would have ratted me out in a heartbeat if I had. I was your typical pain-in-the-ass big brother to her. Anyway, Mom and Dad drove me to the hospital, Dad giving me hell the entire way for destroying his rose bushes, and I spent the rest of the summer in a cast and hobbling around on crutches. It was my one and only time I was successful at sneaking out."

"You call falling out of your window and breaking your ankle, successful?" I said.

"Hey, I got out of the house without them knowing, didn't I?" Wes said. "That counts as successfully sneaking out."

"Fair enough." I rubbed my hand across Wes's chest. "Thanks for letting me crash in your room, Wes. I really appreciate it."

"It's my pleasure." His cock was starting to harden, and I gave him a look of surprise.

"What?" he asked.

"Already?"

He grinned at me. "Impressive, right?"

I shrugged. "It's okay, I guess."

"Okay?" Wes growled playfully before rolling on top of me and pinning me to the bed. He nipped at my neck and then my earlobe. "I guess I need to show you exactly how impressive my dick can be, flower girl."

"Yes, I guess you do, Wesley."

He laughed. "Prepare to be impressed, little flower."

CHAPTER 6

Daisy

"It looks lovely, Daisy. Red is your colour," Frannie's mom said approvingly.

I touched the soft scarf she had wrapped around my neck and said, "Thank you so much for making this for me, Patricia. I really love it."

I swallowed past the lump in my throat and blinked back the tears. I really appreciated her thoughtfulness, and for a moment, I felt a surge of anger at Frannie for making me lie to her mom. She was wonderful and so motherly that it made me miss my own mother with a deep-seated ache that took my breath away.

"Dearest? What's wrong?" Patricia asked.

"Nothing," I said. "I…"

I trailed off, and Patricia said, "You just need a mom hug."

Before I could protest, Patricia had wrapped me in her arms. I hesitated only briefly before returning her hug. God, it felt good to be hugged by a mom again, even if it wasn't my mom. This time, I couldn't stop the tears from dripping down my face. Patricia leaned back and studied me silently before wiping the tears away with her thumbs.

"Frannie told me what happened to your parents," she said. "I'm very sorry, Daisy. The holidays must be a tough time for you."

"A little," I admitted.

"Well," Patricia cleared her throat briskly and wiped at her own eyes, "anytime you need a mom hug, you just ask. Okay?"

"Yeah, okay." I was still crying, and Patricia handed me a tissue as Wes stepped into the living room.

"Dad says if we don't leave in the next five minutes, he's driving to Walmart and buying a fake tree," Wes said.

"He makes that threat every year," Patricia said with a laugh. "He's - "

"Daisy? What's wrong? Why are you crying?" Wes walked toward me. When he reached for me, I gave him a wide-eyed look of warning. He dropped his arms, his face flushing a dull red as he glanced at his mom before stepping back.

Patricia gave us both a considering look that made me very nervous before saying, "Nothing's wrong, honey. Daisy was saying thank you for the scarf."

"Right. Uh, well, we should get going," Wes said. "There isn't enough room in the truck for all of us. Dad said he'd drive the car with you and Grandma, and Frannie and Daisy can go in the truck with me."

"Why don't you let Frannie and Daisy go with Dad?" Patricia said. "It'll give your father a chance to get to know Frannie's girlfriend better."

She put a slight emphasis on Frannie's girlfriend, and my insides churned with guilt and nerves as Wes said, "Sure. I don't care either way."

He sounded convincing enough to me, but his mother

gave him another assessing look before smiling at me. "Ready to go chop down a Christmas tree, Daisy?"

"As long as I'm not the one chopping," I said.

Patricia laughed. "No, dearest. We'll leave that job to Wes."

"WAIT, SO YOU REALLY ARE ALLOWED TO JUST WALK INTO THE woods and cut down a tree?" I asked in confusion.

Frannie's dad nodded. "Yes. It's a tree farm. There are about 200 acres of trees. You can harvest your own, or you can head over to the barn and purchase a pre-cut one."

He pointed to a large red barn with a steady flow of people coming in and out. I wrapped my new scarf more snugly around my neck as Frannie took my hand and squeezed it. "Daisy's a city girl, Dad. She didn't even know tree farms existed. Did you?"

I shook my head as Wes and his mother and grandmother joined us at the edge of the woods. Patricia smiled at her husband. "Okay, so Jim says the price is seventy dollars this year and - "

"Seventy!" Frannie's dad said. "It's gone up twenty bucks."

"Hush now, Gregory," Patricia said. "You know Jim has to provide for his family. They had a third boy three months ago."

Gregory rolled his eyes. "You got the saw, Wes? Hey, earth to Wes!"

Wes dragged his gaze from my and Frannie's clasped hands. "Yes, you see it in my hand, don't you?"

"Don't get smart with me, Wesley," Gregory said with a grin.

"Sorry, sir," Wes said.

Frannie's hand tightened painfully onto mine, and I grimaced before whispering, "Frannie, not so tight."

"Well, isn't this a surprise?" a voice said behind us.

Gregory stiffened and spun around, glaring at the smaller man standing behind him. "What are you doing here, Brenner?"

"Getting a Christmas tree, of course. What else would I be doing here?" the man said with a sardonic grin.

Gregory flushed all over as Patricia hurried over and put her hand on his arm. "We should get going, dearest."

"Hello, Patricia. You're looking lovely," the man said.

"Thank you, Ryan," Patricia said.

"Dad? I checked out the trees in the barn, and I think we should... whoa."

Frannie made a low gasp of delight as Owen jogged up to the group.

"Hello, Owen," Patricia said. "How are you?"

"Good, thanks, Mrs. McKinley. How about yourself?" Owen asked. His gaze drifted to Frannie, and an -admittedly adorable - look of adoration came over his face.

"Fine," Patricia said. Neither Frannie nor Owen noticed the way she watched as Owen approached us.

"Uh, hi. It's Francine, right?" Owen said before holding out his hand.

Frannie, her face a lovely shade of pink, shook Owen's hand. "Frannie, actually."

I discreetly elbowed Frannie in the side when she continued to hold Owen's hand. She stared blankly at me as her mother said, "Frannie, dearest, aren't you going to introduce Daisy to the Brenners?"

"Right, of course," Frannie said as she dropped Owen's hand. "Uh, Owen and Mr. Brenner, this is Daisy."

"Nice to meetcha," Owen said. He grinned at me, and I shook his hand before smiling at his father.

"Hello, Mr. Brenner. It's nice to meet you."

"Likewise," he said.

"Daisy is Frannie's lesbian lover," Frannie's grandmother said. "They have sex together."

"Grandma!"

"Mother Francine!"

Frannie and Patricia made identical shrieks of horror as Wes and Owen burst into laughter. I wondered if my face was as red as Gregory and Mr. Brenner's and decided it probably was.

"What?" her grandmother said. "I heard them having sex last night when I got up to use the bathroom. Frannie's a moaner."

"Grandma, be quiet!" Frannie said.

"Nothing to be ashamed of," her grandmother said.

"Yeah, Frannie, it's nothing to be ashamed of," Wes said teasingly.

His grandmother arched one badly-drawn eyebrow at him. "You're one to talk, Wesley. I heard you last night grunting and groaning, too, you know. You got a girlfriend we don't know about?"

Wes' mouth dropped open, and I wondered if I should confess everything right then and there. I wasn't cut out for a life of lying or lesbianism.

"Grandma, I wasn't… I mean…there was no one in my room last night," Wes said.

"So, you were pullin' your own pickle then, were you?" his grandmother asked.

"Mother, please," Gregory said. "I am begging you to stop talking."

"Why don't we all go to the canteen and we'll grab a nice cup of hot chocolate to drink while we're searching for our tree?" Patricia said.

"Good idea," Gregory muttered. "If we're drinking, we're not talking."

"Can you grab ours, Mom?" Frannie was staring at Owen

again. "Daisy and I want to check out the gift shop in the barn."

"Sure, but don't be long, dearest," Patricia replied.

"We won't." Frannie was still staring at Owen, and I took her hand and squeezed it in warning. She gave me a distracted smile as Patricia watched the two of us.

"Owen, where's your mother?" Mr. Brenner asked.

"Over by the gate, talking to Mrs. Parten." Owen stayed where he was when his father started toward the gate.

"Owen? Let's go."

"Um, I think I'm going to check out the gift shop too," Owen said. "There's a snow globe I'm thinking of buying."

His father sighed irritably. "A snow globe? Since when do you care about snow globes?"

Owen shrugged. "I like snow globes, Dad. Don't make a big deal about it."

"Fine, but don't be long," his father retorted.

"Yeah, okay. Uh, do you ladies mind if I walk over there with you?" Owen asked.

"Not at all." Frannie's voice was too bright and eager, and I squeezed her hand again. She glanced at me before pulling me toward the barn.

"Meet back here in ten minutes," Patricia called after us.

"You bet!" Frannie shouted over her shoulder.

I wondered if Wes was staring at my ass as we walked away and had to resist the urge to turn and check. Hoping he was looking at my ass was stupid. His mother was way too perceptive for her own good, and she'd undoubtedly notice if her kid were checking out his sister's girlfriend's butt.

The minute we were out of earshot, Owen said, "Babe, I miss you so bad."

"I miss you too, baby," Frannie said. "It's killing me not to be with you."

"Weren't you just together last night?" I asked. "It's been like six hours."

"Yeah, but six hours is like six months in Owen and Frannie time," Owen said solemnly.

I rolled my eyes as Frannie grinned like a maniac at Owen. "Can you get away for a bit after this?"

"Probably," Owen said. "I drove my own car here because Mom and Dad are stopping at the Lestons' place."

"Let's meet at the bookstore over on Robinson Street. It'll be quiet there, and they have that little nook near the back. No one will see us."

"Frannie!" I hissed at her. "You cannot have sex with Owen in a bookstore."

"We're not going to," Frannie said.

"We're not?" Owen said.

"No, baby, we're not," Frannie said. "But we can have some alone time together."

"You had alone time last night," I said.

Frannie ignored me. "What do you say, baby?"

"Of course," Owen replied. "You know I can't resist my lady."

"Oh, good!" Frannie said. "So, we should be done here around two. Let's meet at the bookstore at two thirty. I'll have Wes drive me to the bookstore. I'll tell him I'm buying a last-minute gift for Daisy to explain why he has to drive her home instead of dropping her off with me."

"It's a date," Owen said as we approached the open doors of the barn.

"Excuse me," I said, "but are you seriously going to ditch me with your family for the afternoon?"

"My family loves you, Daisy," Frannie said. "Besides, it'll be like an hour or two at the most. Please? I really need time with Owen."

I opened my mouth to tell her absolutely not, but then I

realized something. If Frannie had Wes take us to the bookstore and drop her off, I'd be alone with Wes on the way home. Sure, it wouldn't be for very long, but I'd take what I could get.

"Fine," I said. "But you're being a really bad girlfriend, Frannie."

She laughed and gave me a one-armed hug. "I totally am."

"WHY DO YOU WANT TO DRIVE BACK WITH WES?" PATRICIA asked.

"Because he's my brother and I love him and I don't get to see him all that often?" Frannie said.

Patricia gave her a skeptical look. "Since when do you and Wes even get along?"

"Hey, that's hurtful." Wes' deep voice spoke beside me, and I tried not to look at the way his biceps bulged against his long-sleeve shirt. He had just finished tying down the tree in the back of the truck. Staring at the muscles in his back and arms while he wrestled the tree onto the truck bed had made me shamefully hot. "Frannie and I get along great, Mom."

"No, you don't," Patricia said. "I love you both, but you drive me crazy with your fighting."

"We've turned over a new leaf," Wes said. "I'm making up for all the rotten things I did to Frannie when we were kids and trying to be a good brother. I would be happy to give Frannie and Daisy a ride home."

I could see Frannie giving Wes an odd look, and I wondered if she would question him about his sudden enthusiasm for sibling bonding.

"Yes, you do seem to be rather eager to be alone with them," Patricia said.

My stomach dropped, but Wes just grinned at her before giving her a loud kiss on the cheek. "Like I said, I've got some making up to do."

"That's for sure," Frannie said. "Okay, it's settled. We'll see you at home!"

She grabbed my hand and pulled me toward the truck before her parents and grandmother could argue. "You sit in the middle, Daisy."

She didn't have to ask me twice. I was reaching for the door frame to try to haul myself up when Wes's big hands cupped my hips. He lifted me into the truck as butterflies swarmed to life in my stomach. I mumbled a thank you and moved to the middle. Wes helped Frannie into the truck before sliding behind the driver's seat.

"Ready?" He turned the key, and the truck rumbled to life.

"Yes." Frannie glanced at her phone. "Hurry up, would you, Wes?"

"Do you have somewhere to be?" he asked.

"Actually," Frannie gave him a look that would melt butter, "would you mind dropping me off at the Books For All bookstore?"

"What for?"

"I have a last-minute gift I need to pick up for my girl." Frannie put her hand on my knee and gave it a gentle squeeze. "It's like fifteen minutes out of your way, Wes. Drop me off and I'll catch an Uber home."

"All right," Wes said.

Frannie twitched on the seat next to me. I knew she'd been gearing up for Wes to balk at her request, and I had to bite back my giggle at the look of astonishment on her face.

"Really?" she said. "Just like that?"

"Yes," Wes said.

"Huh, I thought you were screwing with Mom when you said all that crap about being a better brother."

"Maybe you could try being a better sister," Wes said with a grin. "Meet me halfway."

"Sorry, Wesley, not gonna happen," Frannie replied. "Your face bugs me too much."

Wes and I both burst into laughter, and after a moment, Frannie joined in.

Wes

THE MINUTE FRANNIE HAD DISAPPEARED INTO THE BOOKSTORE, I patted the seat beside me. "Slide back over here, Daisy."

She had moved to the passenger seat when Frannie hopped out of the truck, and I missed her soft warmth. She hesitated and glanced at the street. "What if someone sees us?"

"They won't. Come sit next to me, darlin'," I coaxed.

She slid over until her thigh was pressed against mine. I pulled out onto the street and then took her hand, linking our fingers as I drove.

"So, is Frannie actually buying you a gift, or is she meeting Owen?" I asked.

"She's meeting Owen," Daisy said. "They came up with the idea at the tree farm."

"Did they plan that meeting too?"

"Nope, that was a happy coincidence." She shivered against me when I rubbed my thumb across the palm of her hand. "I almost died when your grandma said she heard you last night."

I laughed. "You and me both. I think I covered pretty well."

"You definitely didn't," she said. "Your mom knows something weird is going on."

"She doesn't. Don't worry, Daisy. Besides, we'll just have to be quieter next time."

She didn't reply, and I cursed inwardly. Assuming there would be a next time was stupid of me. For all I knew, Daisy was done with me. The thought made the hot chocolate in my stomach curdle. God, I was falling for this girl and falling fast. I needed to slow things down before I made a complete fool of myself. We lived in different cities, and she was Frannie's roommate. Frannie would lose her shit if Daisy and I started dating. Not to mention how confusing it would be for the rest of the family.

I cleared my throat as Daisy peered out the windshield. "Where are we?"

"I thought I would take the scenic route home," I said.

Her smile made my pulse speed up. "The scenic route, huh?"

"Yes." I let go of her hand and placed mine on her thigh instead. I rubbed her leg through her jeans as she studied my hand. I wondered if she was remembering the last time we were alone in the truck together.

"Thinking about being inappropriate, Mr. McKinley?" She said.

"Do you want me to be inappropriate?" I asked as I tried to move my hand between her thighs.

"Hey, eyes on the road, both hands on the wheel," she admonished.

I did what she asked. My disappointment turned to red-hot need the minute I felt her hand rest on my crotch. My cock immediately hardened, and she made her adorable little laugh before squeezing me. "You're insatiable, Wes."

"You do that to me," I rasped.

When she unbuttoned and unzipped my jeans and stuck her hand down my briefs, I made a low groan and thrust against her soft hand. Her warm fingers curled around my cock and stroked back and forth. I tried desperately to concentrate on the road, thankful that there was hardly any traffic.

"Do you know what I want, Wes?" Daisy leaned against me, and I groaned when her warm tongue traced my ear.

"What?" I gasped as she rubbed her thumb over the head of my aching cock.

"I want to taste you," she breathed into my ear.

"Fuck, yes," I said.

Daisy let out a soft shriek as I abruptly turned the truck left, throwing her against me. Her hand tightened on my dick, and dammit if I didn't almost come all over her hand right there. I held onto my self-control with grim determination as I drove down the side street.

"Where are we going?" Daisy asked.

"You'll see." I pulled her hand out of my pants and smiled at her when she pouted.

"Trust me, darlin', if I don't do this, we'll get in a car accident. I don't relish the idea of explaining to my mother why the paramedics found us with your hand in my pants."

She laughed and leaned her head against my shoulder. "All right. I'll stop teasing you."

I drove another ten minutes until we were at the old warehouse on the edge of town. It had been abandoned for years, and Daisy leaned forward and peered out the windshield. Most of the windows were broken, and graffiti was painted across the building.

"It's kind of creepy out here," Daisy said.

"It isn't," I said. "It's nice and private, and I need privacy for what I'm going to do to you."

"What are you going to do to me?" She asked with a sweet smile.

I cupped the back of her neck and pulled her toward me. We kissed, our tongues touching and tasting until we were both panting. I cupped her breast through her heavy jacket, growling when I couldn't feel her nipple.

"Take off your jacket," I demanded.

She shrugged out of it as I pulled mine off as well. We tossed them on the seat beside her, and she moaned when I cupped her breast again. I teased her nipple through her bra and t-shirt as we kissed repeatedly.

"You taste so good, little flower," I said.

"You too," she panted. "Like chocolate."

I grinned at her, but it dropped like a stone a few seconds later. "Shit."

"What's wrong?" she asked. She was starting to work her hand into my jeans again.

"I don't have a condom with me."

She laughed. "This is about you, anyway."

"What do you mean?" God, I hoped she meant what I thought she did.

She slipped her hand back into my briefs and rubbed my still-hard cock. "You know what I mean."

"Fuck!" My breath escaped in a low moan when she pushed the front of my briefs down. I watched her tiny hand rub my cock as she smiled at me.

"Have you ever had a blow job in the car before, Wes?"

"No," I groaned.

Her hand slowed to a stop, and I gave her a pleading look. "Fuck, Daisy. Don't stop."

"You've seriously never had a girlfriend give you road head?" she asked.

"No. I never had one offer, and I didn't want to ask. It seemed," I searched for the appropriate word, "disrespectful."

"Oh my God, you're adorable," she said with a soft laugh.

"Are women waiting for men to ask them to blow them in the car?" I said. "Because I am more than happy to beg - I mean - ask if you - "

ELIZABETH KELLY

"Shut up, Wes." She leaned over and sucked my dick into her mouth.

"Fuck, yes!" I hissed. My hands tangled in her soft hair as she bobbed her head up and down my dick. Her mouth was hot and wet, and I groaned in sheer delight when she used her tongue to trace circles around the head. Pre-cum was already leaking out of my dick, and I watched as she licked it away before smiling up at me.

"Yummy."

I twitched and pushed her mouth over my dick again. "Suck, darlin'."

I let my head drop back against the seat, closing my eyes as she went to town on my dick. Daisy was a fucking goddess at sucking dick, and I thrust into her mouth as she sucked and licked and drove me crazy. I had no idea how much time had passed. My focus was narrowed down to the feel of Daisy's hot mouth and tongue. Her hand was stroking the base of my cock as she made slow and almost lazy licks along the shaft.

"Please," I rasped. "Oh, please, darlin'."

She slid her mouth over my cock and made a humming sound. It vibrated against my flesh, and I pulled her off my dick in a hurry.

"What's wrong?" she asked.

"I'm close. You're so fucking good at this," I moaned.

"Oh, honey, you haven't seen anything yet."

"What do you – oh fucking hell!" I made a hoarse bellow of pleasure as Daisy slid her mouth down over my dick until her lips touched my pubic hair. I'd never once been deepthroated before, and as Daisy pulled back, took a deep breath and then deepthroated me again, I climaxed explosively. Her throat worked as she swallowed, and I pumped my cock repeatedly into her mouth as she swallowed every drop of my cum. When she finally sat up and wiped her

86

mouth with the heel of her hand, I was shaking and weak as a kitten.

"You okay?" she asked.

"Marry me," I said hoarsely.

Her laughter filled me with warmth, and I wanted to pull her into my lap and hug her, but the steering wheel was in the way, and I could barely lift my damn arms. I settled for patting her weakly on the leg.

She laughed again before lifting my arm and snuggling under it. I stroked her hip and side as she rested her head on my shoulder. After I caught my breath, I said, "That was hands down the best blow job of my life, Daisy."

"Good," she said.

"I'm sorry I didn't warn you," I said. "I didn't know I was going to come."

"It's fine," she said. "Nice girls always swallow anyway."

"You're the perfect woman," I said.

She giggled and patted my chest. "Aren't you sweet."

It was obvious she thought I was being flippant. I wanted to tell her I meant every word of it, but hell, what if I really was just on a post-orgasmic high? Besides, I had more important matters to take care of, like making Daisy come all over my fingers.

"Daisy?"

She lifted her head, and I kissed her. I could taste myself on her tongue, and fuck if it didn't make me horny again. "Your turn," I whispered against her mouth.

"You don't have to," she said.

"I want to," I replied. I stuck my hand under her shirt, but before I could cup her breast, my cell phone rang. I muttered a curse. It was my mother's ringtone.

"Wes?" Daisy said when I pulled my phone out of my pocket.

"I have to answer it," I said. "It's Mom."

She rested her head against my chest again as I answered the call.

"Hey, Mom."

"Wes? Where are you?"

"On our way home, why?"

"I thought you'd been in an accident. Do you have any idea what time it is?" Mom asked.

I glanced at my watch. Fuck, we'd been parked at the old warehouse for nearly forty minutes.

"Oh, uh, sorry. Frannie asked me to drop her off at Books For All so she could pick up a gift for Daisy."

"Are you waiting for her?" Mom asked.

"No, she said she'd be awhile and she'd find her own way home," I said without thinking.

"Then where the heck are you? We've been waiting for you for nearly an hour."

"Um…"

Daisy sat up and made a "think of something" motion with her hand.

"We, uh…" Fuck, my mind was a complete blank. I was pretty sure Daisy had sucked most of my brain cells right out of me.

"Wesley? Where have you been?" My mother said impatiently.

"Um, I'm driving, Mom, so I'd better go," I said. "We'll be home soon."

I hit the end button before she could reply and stared at Daisy.

"That was not so smooth," she said.

"I panicked. My mind went blank!" I said. "I'm lucky I didn't blurt out the truth."

"Oh God," Daisy said with a laugh. "That would have been a nightmare."

"Yep," I said before reaching for the button on her jeans.

She slapped my hand away. "What are you doing?"

"I'll make you come and then we'll leave," I said.

"Like hell you are! Wes, we need to get to your house now."

I scowled at her. "I'm not in the habit of leaving my woman unsatisfied, Daisy."

A weird look crossed her face, and I said, "What?"

"Nothing," she said. "I appreciate the thought, but we have to go, right now. Is there a coffee shop on the way home?"

"Yes," I said as I buttoned and zipped my jeans. "Why?"

"Because I have an idea. Let's go."

I could see how impatient she was, but I took a moment to kiss her anyway. "Thank you, Daisy. You're incredible."

She gave me a pleased smile. "Thanks, Wes. Now drive!"

CHAPTER 7

Wes

"Daisy, it was so sweet of you to stop and get us all coffees," my mother said as she opened a large plastic tub with "Christmas" written across the top of it.

"It was my pleasure, Patricia," Daisy said. "I'm sorry it made you worry. I wanted to surprise you, but it was so busy at the coffee shop we should have texted you and told you we'd be delayed."

"Oh, it's fine," Mom said. "Although I can't believe Frannie still isn't back."

"She texted me ten minutes ago," Daisy said. "She ran into a friend and is having a coffee with her."

"Which friend?" My grandmother asked. She was sitting on the couch, drinking her coffee and watching as Dad and I strung the lights around the tree.

"She didn't say," Daisy replied. "Patricia, does this tub have ornaments as well?"

"Yes, dearest," my mother replied. "Go ahead and open that one. Love, are you almost finished with the lights?"

"We are," my father replied. "Wes, crawl under the tree and plug the lights in, would you?"

I did what he asked and then crawled back out, dusting the pine needles off the knees of my jeans. Daisy was bent over the plastic tub in front of her as she sorted through it, and I stared appreciatively at her ass. God, she had amazing tits and a nice, firm ass. I needed to get her alone so I could give her an orgasm. It was killing me that I'd had one and she didn't.

"Oh shoot, we should add some water to the tree before we start decorating," my mother said. "Wes, can you get some water, please?"

I tore my gaze from Daisy's ass. "Sure."

My grandmother was staring at me, and I groaned inwardly. No doubt she'd seen me leering at Daisy's ass. Fuck, I really needed better self-control. I headed toward the kitchen, determined to do a better job at keeping my eyes to myself and my distance from Daisy when my family was around.

FRANNIE RETURNED JUST BEFORE DINNER, AND DAISY MUST have texted her the cover story because she didn't hesitate when Mom asked her who she'd run into.

"Leslie Warburger," she said. "We went to high school together."

"I know who she is," Mom said. "Did you have a nice visit?"

"We did," Frannie said as she sat down at the island next to Daisy. She had a small bag in her hand, and she set it on the top of the island. "When are we decorating the tree?"

"We already did," I said.

"You didn't wait for me?" She gave Mom a hurt look.

"Why would she when her favourite kid was there to help," I said. "That's what happens when you ditch us for Leslie Warburger."

"Shut up, Wesley," she retorted. "Mom, you should have waited."

My mother shrugged. "I didn't think you would mind that much. Sorry, honey. I'm making my famous gingerbread cookies tomorrow. You can help me with that."

"Okay, but only me," Frannie said.

"And Daisy," Mom said.

"What?" Frannie gave her a blank look.

"Your girlfriend, dearest. You don't want to exclude her, do you?"

Frannie flushed before putting her arm around Daisy and giving her a brief kiss on the mouth. "Of course not. Daisy knows I want her there. It's Wes I don't want around."

She stuck her tongue out at me as I glared at her. Jealousy was niggling at my spine, and I tried to ignore it. Even though I knew it was an act, it bugged me when Frannie touched Daisy.

"Like I want to hang around my bratty little sister, anyway," I said.

"At least my birth certificate isn't an apology letter from a condom company," Frannie said.

Daisy started laughing, and I couldn't help but join in. Frannie had always been better than me at insults.

"I see the 'turning over a new leaf' is going well," my mother said as she sliced tomatoes for the salad.

I kissed her cheek and stole a slice of tomato. "Your favourite child will be in the living room with Dad if you need him."

My resolve to keep my distance from Daisy lasted until after dinner. All of us were sitting in the living room watching a movie when Daisy excused herself. I waited a couple of minutes and, when it was apparent that the rest of my family was engrossed in the movie, silently slipped out of the living room.

I found Daisy in the kitchen, pouring herself a glass of water. Before she could say anything, I took her hand and pulled her into the walk-in pantry. I shut the door and flicked on the light before pushing her back against the built-in shelves.

"Wes? What are you doing?" she said before eyeing the door nervously. "Your family's in the living room."

"I know," I said. "So, you'll have to be quiet."

"Quiet about what?"

I grinned at her. She had changed into yoga pants and a t-shirt after dinner, and the elastic waistband made it simple for me to push my hand past her pants and under her panties. I was cupping her warm pussy, my fingers stroking her clit before her hand had even wrapped around my forearm.

"Wes!" she said as her nails dug into my skin. "Stop that!"

"Stop what? This?" I rubbed her clit with the hard strokes I knew would make her hot, and was rewarded with a soft moan.

"Shh," I said before kissing her. She returned my kiss eagerly, but when I released her mouth, she gave me a nervous look.

"We shouldn't do this right now."

I rubbed her clit again. "Yes, we should. I won't be able to sleep tonight if I don't make sure you're satisfied, little flower."

"Oh!" she gasped. She was growing steadily wetter, and I used some of her moisture to help ease my finger into her tight pussy. She clenched around me, and my dick hardened. I pressed it against her hip.

"Fuck, I love it when you squeeze like that," I whispered into her ear. "Lift your shirt, darlin'."

"Wes, we shouldn't," she moaned.

"Lift your shirt and show me your beautiful tits," I repeated.

She lifted her shirt, and I admired her pink lacy bra before prompting her, "Daisy, show me."

She glanced at the door to the pantry before unhooking the front clasp of her bra and peeling back the cups.

"Beautiful," I whispered before bending my head. Her nipples were already hard, and I sucked on the right one as I pushed a second finger into her. I finger fucked her with slow strokes until she pulled on my hair and made a pleading sound.

I could have teased her all night, but my family would eventually notice we were both gone. Still fucking her with my fingers, I angled my thumb over her clit and rubbed hard as I placed my mouth to her ear.

"You're so tight around my fingers. I wish it were my cock you were squeezing."

"Oh God," she moaned. "Maybe we could have a quickie."

I shook my head and traced her ear with my tongue. "Not enough time, darlin'."

"Please, Wes," she pleaded as I used my left hand to pull and pinch at her nipples.

"No, little flower. But the next time we fuck, I'll give you my cock for as long as you need it."

"Do you promise?" she whimpered. She ground her pussy against my hand with desperate need.

"I promise," I said. "I'm going to put you on your hands and knees and fuck you until you come all over my cock."

"Oh my God," she whispered as she rose onto her tiptoes before grinding against me again. "Oh God, I'm so close."

"Good," I said.

"You're so good at touching me," she moaned. "God, I love it when you touch me."

"I love it too, darlin'. Now show me how pretty you look when you're coming all over my fingers." I pulled my fingers out of her and pulled on her clit with a short, hard tug as I covered her mouth with mine.

I swallowed her moan of pleasure, stroking my tongue against hers as she climaxed against my fingers. I could feel her nipples pressing against my chest through my shirt, and I rubbed my dick along her hip as she shuddered before collapsing against me.

I held her up and pressed kisses along her jaw and over her temple as I rubbed her back with my left hand and eased my other hand out of her pants.

"Oh my God," she whispered. "That was so good."

I nuzzled her throat, then helped her back into her bra before smoothing down her shirt. "Better get back to the living room before they notice we're both gone."

"Right," she said.

I kissed her again, and she squeezed my ass before walking a bit unsteadily to the door of the pantry and opening it. As she stepped into the kitchen, my grandmother's voice immediately made me lose my erection.

"Daisy? Why were you in the pantry?"

"Mrs. McKinley!" Daisy's voice was high-pitched and anxious. "Hi."

"You can call me grandma," my grandmother said. "What were you doing in the pantry?"

"Oh, I was um…." Daisy's voice trailed off, and I grabbed a bag of chips from the top shelf and headed toward the door.

"Daisy? I found the chips. You don't have to ask Mom – oh, hey, Grandma."

"What are you doing in the pantry with Daisy?" Grandma asked.

"Looking for chips." I held them up. "Did you want some too?"

She studied us for a moment. Daisy's cheeks were flushed, and I wondered if Grandma could see the way her body was quivering. God, I hoped not.

"No, thank you," my grandmother finally said. "I wanted a cup of tea."

"Okay." I tossed the bag of chips to Daisy, who fumbled it and nearly dropped the bag. "I'm going to use the bathroom. Can you take these to the living room for me?"

"Sure," Daisy said. She left the kitchen without looking at us.

I was about to follow her when Grandma called my name.

"What's up, Grannie Frannie?" I said.

She ignored my childhood nickname for her. "I know you and your sister don't always get along, but you love her. Don't you, Wesley?"

"Of course I do," I said.

"Then don't do anything that will break her heart."

"I won't."

Grandma stepped closer, and I tucked my hands behind my back as she reached up and patted me on the cheek. "You've always been a good boy, Wesley. Stay that way."

"Yes, ma'am," I said.

Daisy

I suppose I shouldn't have been surprised when I walked into Frannie's bedroom and found her making out with Owen on the bed. I shut the door as they sat up, and Frannie gave me a guilty look.

"Do you mind if Owen spends the night with me again?"

I cheered inwardly as I arranged a scowl on my face. "Seriously, Frannie? You just saw him today."

"But we didn't get to bone," Owen said.

I rolled my eyes as Frannie said, "I miss him, Daisy."

"Fine," I sighed. "I'll sleep in the basement. But be quieter this time."

"I will!" Frannie said happily. "Thanks, honey. You're the best!"

I nodded and grabbed my phone before heading out into the hallway. It was quiet and dark, and I tiptoed my way down the hall to Wes's room. Afraid his parents would hear if I knocked, I opened the door and slipped inside.

The sky was clouded over tonight, so no moonlight shone into his room. It was pitch black, and I closed the door with a quiet click. I could hear Wes groaning softly, and I whispered, "Wes?"

"Shit!" I could hear him fumbling for the light next to his bed, and I blinked and squinted when he clicked it on.

"Daisy?" he said in a harsh whisper. "You scared the hell out of me."

"Sorry, I didn't want to knock in case your parents heard." My gaze drifted down his naked chest to where the covers concealed his crotch. His erection was obvious, and I flushed a little before saying, "Were you masturbating?"

"Yes," he said shamelessly.

"Oh my God," I said. "Wes!"

He shrugged. "I started thinking about how hot you looked when you came all over my hand in the pantry."

"Your grandmother almost caught us," I said.

"Keep talking about my grandma, and I'm gonna lose my erection," he said.

I tried not to giggle as I gave him a disapproving look. "That was a very dangerous idea."

"Like I told you before, I don't like leaving my woman unsatisfied."

A thrill went through me. That was the second time that Wes had referred to me as his woman. It probably didn't mean anything, but damn, did I like hearing it. More than I should have.

"So, Owen is in Frannie's room again, and I need a place to sleep," I said.

He threw back the covers. "Climb in, darlin'. But I should warn you now – you won't be sleeping."

My stomach quivered with anticipation as I crawled over his legs and sat next to him. "Is that a fact?"

"Yes, ma'am." Wes waited patiently as I set my phone alarm for six-thirty. He placed my phone on the nightstand and then reached for my nightdress. I let him pull it over my head without protest.

He cupped my breasts and teased my nipples as we kissed. When I was panting and moaning, he pulled back and smiled at me. "You're beautiful, Daisy."

"Thank you. So are you."

His fingers were tracing my appendectomy scar, and I moaned again when he pushed his hand into my panties and tugged on the curls.

"I really do love your sweet little pussy," he said as his fingers found my clit. He rubbed me until I was wet and swollen - shamefully, it didn't take very long – watching my face as I bit at my lip and tried to keep my voice down.

"Oh God, that's so good."

I wasn't lying to him. After years of always having to make myself climax, Wes's skill at touching me was a drug I

ELIZABETH KELLY

couldn't resist. He gave my clit a hard pinch that sent elec-
tricity zapping down my spine.

"Wes?" I whispered.

"Yeah?" He was kissing the top of my shoulder with his
warm mouth.

"Can I ask you a question?"

It probably wasn't the best time to ask, but I needed to
know. Wes was the only guy who'd figured out that I needed
a rough, sometimes downright hard, touch to orgasm, and I
was afraid he might think I was a freak.

"Mm-hmm," he replied as he tasted the hollow of my
throat.

"Do you think I'm a freak because I like to be touched
kind of rough?" I said it in a fast whisper, trying not to panic
when his fingers slowed on my clit.

He raised his head, and my anxiety eased when he said,
"No. Not at all."

"Okay, good," I said.

"You're perfectly normal, Daisy."

"Am I?" I asked. "You're the first guy I've been with who
can make me come. That isn't normal."

"You're normal," he insisted. "The other men you've slept
with were terrible at fucking."

"You don't know that," I laughed.

"They didn't make you come," he said. "They're terrible at
fucking."

"I think it freaked them out when I kept asking for," I
hesitated, "a rougher touch."

He rolled his eyes. "Darlin', you could ask me to spank
you and I still wouldn't think you were a freak."

"Have you spanked a woman before?" I asked.

"No, have you?"

I laughed so hard that Wes pressed his hand over my
mouth until my laughter subsided. "No, I've never spanked a

woman or a man before. For the record, I'm pretty positive I don't want to be spanked, so don't get any ideas. But I will spank you if you ask nicely."

"Sweet," Wes said. "I'm a lucky man."

That made me laugh again, and this time Wes stopped the laughter by kissing me. I reached under the covers and stroked his cock until he groaned into my mouth. He stopped rubbing my clit, and I whimpered in protest. He ignored it as he pulled my panties down my legs and tossed them on the floor.

"On your hands and knees," he said.

My pussy quivered, and I moved onto my hands and knees as Wes rolled a condom onto his cock. He kneeled behind me, and I arched my back when he ran his warm hand over my butt.

"You have a really great ass," he said in a low voice.

"Thank you," I moaned.

He traced the backs of my thighs with his fingertips, sending little shivers up and down my spine. "Spread your legs wide, little flower."

I did what he asked, holding my breath with anticipation as he moved closer. He grasped my hips and rearranged me – God, I loved how strong he was – before pressing the head of his cock against my entrance.

Without saying anything, he pushed into me until I felt his pelvis press against my ass. I bit back my moan as I stretched around his thick cock. His big hand rubbed my lower back, and he waited patiently for me to adjust.

"Good?" He asked.

"Yes," I said.

I tried not to moan too loudly when Wes began a slow, steady rhythm. He pressed on my upper back, and I rested my chest against the bed and buried my face in his pillow to muffle my cries of pleasure.

Wes was moving harder now, rocking me into the bed with every thrust as he bottomed out, then pulled back until just the head of his cock was inside of me. He thrust again, and I squeezed around his dick, pulling a moan of delight from his throat.

"Fuck, darlin', you have no idea how tight you are," he murmured.

He leaned forward and wound one hand in my hair, pulling until I moved back to my hands. He pulled again, making my back arch and holding me steady as he pounded into me. I wouldn't be able to come this way, but I didn't care. I felt powerful and beautiful as Wes moaned and his hand tightened in my hair. He was close. I could already recognize his signs. I thrust back against him with frenzied enthusiasm as he dropped his hand to my shoulder and held me in a firm grip. I almost squealed out loud when I felt his other hand cup my pussy and rub my clit.

He touched me exactly the way I needed him to, and I buried my face in my upper arm to dampen my moans as he pushed me closer to climax. The sound of our bodies slapping together was too loud, but I barely noticed. I needed to come, I needed Wes to fuck me hard until I was screaming his name. Nothing else mattered but my orgasm.

I closed my eyes, rocking my pelvis hard against Wes's big body as my climax exploded inside of me and I screamed into my arm. Dimly, I could hear Wes's low groan as both of his hands clamped around my hips and he held me still. His body arched, and we shook and moaned in unison until my arms gave out and I collapsed face-first into the mattress.

Wes pulled out and rolled onto his side beside me. His chest heaved as he gasped for air. "You...okay?"

I gave him a weak thumbs-up before curling onto my side. Wes fumbled to remove the condom as I closed my eyes and listened to my pulse pounding in my ears. When he spooned me, cupping my breast with his warm hand and kissing the back of my shoulder, I sighed happily.

"That was really good, little flower," he mumbled against my skin.

"Mm, hmm," I whispered. "Night, Wes."

"Night, Daisy."

CHAPTER 8

Daisy

"Frannie, dearest, try to slice the cheese a bit straighter, please." Patricia stirred the gravy bubbling in a pot on the stove.

"It's the Bakers having dinner with us, not the Pope." Frannie popped a piece of cheese into her mouth before turning and throwing a slice at me. I was standing at the island arranging raw veggies on a platter. I caught the cheese and ate a bite from the slice as Frannie turned back to the cheese sitting on the counter. "They're not going to care if the cheese slices are crooked."

"It's Christmas Eve dinner, and I want everything to look perfect," Patricia said as Wes entered the kitchen.

My pulse immediately sped up, and I could feel my cheeks flushing. Owen had shown up in Frannie's room for the last three nights, and each time, I had feigned annoyance before skipping off to Wes's room. I was addicted to his touch and the way it felt when we had sex.

Just the sex? Or are you addicted to Wes in general?

I ignored my inner voice as Wes stood next to me. He plucked the rest of the cheese from my hand and ate it, grinning at me when I gave him a mock scowl, before leaning against the island. The island was high enough that my lower body was hidden behind it. I almost fell over when I felt Wes's left hand slip under the bottom of my dress and grab my ass. He caressed it gently as he took a piece of carrot from the platter in front of me.

I froze in fear when Patricia turned from the stove. Wes stopped rubbing my ass, but continued to cup it as Patricia said, "Hi, honey. Where's your dad?"

"Down in the basement. Supper smells good."

"Thank you. I'm making your favourite – roast beef."

"Why are you making his favourite?" Frannie asked.

"Because I'm her favourite," Wes said. "How many times do I have to tell you that, Frannie-pants?"

"Don't call me that," Frannie said with a scowl.

She was still slicing up cheese, but she turned to stare at me when her mother said, "Daisy, are you feeling all right? You look flushed."

"I'm fine," I said as Wes squeezed my ass.

"Maybe it's because Wes is practically standing on top of her," Frannie said. "God, Wes, give my girl a little space, would you? She doesn't need you looming over her like that."

Wes squeezed my ass a final time before stepping away. "Sorry, Daisy. I didn't mean to invade your personal space." He gave me an adorable grin. "I really love my vegetables."

"Since when?" Frannie scoffed.

"Since always." Wes grabbed a celery stick and crunched it down.

"Why did you invite the Bakers for dinner tonight?" Frannie asked her mom. "You and Dad aren't friends with them."

"Of course we are," Patricia said. "They sit in the same row as us in church."

"That doesn't make you friends," Frannie said.

"Well, it's nice to make new friends," Patricia said. She was clearly flustered as she wiped her hands on her apron. "Daisy, if you're done with the veggie platter, can you take it to the dining room? You can put it on the table and, if you wouldn't mind, grab the china from the cabinet and start setting the table."

"No problem," I said.

"I'll carry the platter," Wes said. "It looks heavy."

"Daisy doesn't need your help carrying a vegetable platter," Frannie said. "She's not a weakling."

"It's called being a gentleman," Wes said as he picked up the platter. "After you, Daisy."

"Thank you, honey," Patricia said as Wes followed me out of the kitchen. "Set the table for nine, please."

"Nine?" I heard Frannie say. "Why nine? Mr. and Mrs. Baker make eight."

I didn't hear Patricia's reply. Wes was right behind me, and I was distracted by the smell of his aftershave. God, he smelled good.

The dining room was next to the living room. Wes set the vegetable platter on the table as I crossed the room to the china cabinet. I had just opened the doors when Wes's arm slipped around my waist and he pulled me back against him. He nuzzled my neck and cupped my breast, kneading it lightly.

"Wes, behave!" I whispered.

"You look very pretty in your dress, little flower," he said.

"Thank you," I said.

"Wear it to my room tonight so I can take it off you."

"One – Frannie would be suspicious if I went to bed

107

wearing my dress, and two – Owen won't be sneaking into her room tonight," I said. "It's Christmas Eve, remember?"

His hand stilled on my breast, and I heard the disappointment in his voice when he said, "Yeah, I guess that makes sense."

"I'm sorry," I said.

"Me too."

He turned me around and slipped both his arms around my waist before kissing me. I returned his kiss even though I knew it was stupid and dangerous. Any one of Frannie's family could come walking in, but I couldn't resist. Knowing that I wouldn't be in Wes's bed tonight was bumming me out. I'd grown used to sleeping against his warm, hard body.

Wes pulled back and cupped my face, rubbing his thumb along my swollen bottom lip. "I should have given you your Christmas present last night."

"You got me a present? I didn't get you anything," I said.

"You didn't have to," he said, "but now I don't know when I'll give it to you. You and Frannie leave the twenty-sixth, right?"

I nodded. "Yeah. Maybe Owen will sneak over tomorrow night."

"Let's hope," Wes said.

He was bending his head to kiss me again when we heard Frannie's voice drifting down the hall. "I told you, Mom, your pumpkin pie is amazing, and everyone loves it. Don't worry about it."

Wes pulled away from me, and I quickly turned and grabbed some plates from the cabinet. I handed them to Wes as Frannie walked into the room.

"Daisy, do you know – you still haven't set the table?"

She joined us at the china cabinet and gave Wes a friendly shove. "Get your ass moving, Wes. The Bakers will be here any minute, and you still need to change."

Wes studied his t-shirt and jeans. "Why do I need to change?"

"Because you look like a homeless person," Frannie said. "Go put on a different shirt, for God's sake."

She suddenly stopped and sniffed at me before glaring at Wes. "Jesus, Wes, how close were you standing to Daisy? I can smell your aftershave all over her."

I immediately blushed, but Wes was saved from coming up with an excuse by Patricia's entering the dining room. She stared at the three of us crowded around the china cabinet before studying the empty table.

"Do you think that with the three of you, the table might get set before dinner starts?" she asked.

"Sorry, Patricia," I said.

"It's fine, dearest," she said. "Wes, go and change your shirt, please. Put on one with a collar."

"Not you too," Wes said. "What's wrong with my shirt?"

"Just do as I say, please and don't argue," Patricia said. "The Bakers will be here any minute."

"Fine." Wes set the stack of plates on the table before leaving the room.

Frannie opened the drawer to the cabinet and began to pick out the silverware. "Wes is gonna be pissed, Mom. Cheryl isn't his type."

"Oh, hush, he won't be. Besides, Cheryl has changed a lot since high school. You'll see." Patricia hurried out of the room.

"Who's Cheryl?" I asked.

Frannie laughed. "She's the Bakers' daughter. She went to high school with Wes, and she's still single. It's why Mom's invited them tonight for dinner – she's doing her match-making thing."

My stomach dropped, and I abruptly turned and started

setting the plates at the table. "Do you think Wes will like her?"

"God, no," Frannie said. "Cheryl isn't what you would call blessed in the looks department, you know? Not that Wes is shallow about looks – you should have seen his last girl-friend, God, did that girl have a nose on her – but Cheryl was always kind of a bitch."

"Oh yeah?" I wondered if Frannie could hear the relief in my voice."

"Yep. Normally, ugly girls are super sweet because they can't use their looks to get what they want, but not Cheryl," Frannie said with casual cruelty. "I can't wait to see the look on Wes's face when she shows up here tonight. She had a crush on Wes when we were kids."

She suddenly rolled her eyes. "Of course, who didn't have a crush on Wes when we were growing up. It was really gross watching all my friends go gaga over him. He's not even that good looking. It's because he was always nice to my friends when other boys his age wouldn't give them the time of day."

"Your brother is a good guy," I said.

Frannie nodded. "Yep, he is. He drives me crazy, and sometimes I want to punch him in the face, but I love him. When push comes to shove, he always has my back."

She began placing the silverware next to the plate, giving me an evil grin. "Want to make a bet with me on how long it takes Wes to figure out Mom's trying to set him up with Cheryl? The guy is completely obtuse about shit like that. I say he doesn't figure it out until after dessert. What's your guess?"

Still feeling a little sick to my stomach, I shrugged. "I don't know your brother well enough to make it a fair bet."

Frannie gave me a curious look. "You okay, honey? You look pale."

"I'm fine," I said with a forced smile. "It's all good, Frannie."

"Okay." Frannie stopped what she was doing and pulled me into her embrace for a hug. "Thank you again for doing this, honey. I know it's been a real pain in the butt for you, especially sneaking down to the basement every night, but I so appreciate it. I love you lots, Oopsie."

"I love you too, Frannie."

She leaned back and pushed a strand of hair back from my face. "You won't have to sneak to the basement tonight. I promise."

"That's great," I said. Frannie returned to the silverware, and I looked out the window as disappointment flooded through me. I was pretty sure Owen wouldn't be in Frannie's room tonight, but now I had confirmation of it. I hadn't realized until this moment how strongly I'd been holding out hope that I'd have an excuse to go to Wes tonight.

I sighed and moved to the cabinet to get the glasses. It was only one night. Owen was too much of a horndog to go two nights in a row without Frannie. Maybe I wouldn't see Wes tonight, but I'd be back in his bed by tomorrow night.

Yeah, and then you're leaving for home. What then? Even if Frannie eventually comes clean to her parents about dating Owen, if you think she won't be pissed that you're dating her brother, you're fooling yourself. Besides, how would you explain it to the rest of the family?

I rubbed at my temples before grabbing a couple of wine glasses. I didn't want to think about any of that. All I wanted to think about was how good I felt when I was in Wes's arms. If we got the chance to be together tomorrow night, I'd talk to him and see if he was interested in dating. If he wasn't, then none of the other issues mattered.

Wes

I SHOULD HAVE KNOWN MY MOTHER WAS UP TO SOMETHING the minute she told me to change my shirt. But I was wrapped up in trying to think of a way to convince Daisy to come to my room tonight anyway. It was stupid, but the thought of sleeping without her next to me was driving me crazy.

Stupidly, I didn't even clue in when the Bakers first arrived. When mom ushered them into the living room, I was staring at Daisy's legs and thinking about how it felt when I was deep inside of her with those long legs wrapped around my waist.

"Wes!" My mother said in a sharp voice.

I dragged my mind out of the gutter and stood up, giving her an apologetic look before reaching to shake Mr. Baker's hand. "Hello, Mr. and Mrs. Baker. It's nice to see you again."

The older man laughed and gave my hand a hard shake. "I think you're old enough to call us Ralph and Josie now, Wesley."

I nodded and shook Mrs. Baker's hand as my mother said, "You remember their daughter Cheryl. Don't you, Wes?"

A woman stepped out from behind Mr. Baker, and my jaw dropped. "Cheryl?"

"Hello, Wes." Her voice was the same, a low purr designed to make men forget everything but what it would be like to be in her bed, and her eyes were still a shocking bright blue. But everything else was completely different. She looked nothing like the Cheryl I remembered.

I twitched in surprise when I reached to shake her hand, and she brushed past it and hugged me instead. She'd been on the thin side in high school with small breasts and no ass to speak of. Now, her breasts were at least a triple D, and they looked almost obscene on her small frame.

"It's been a long time," she said. "You look terrific," she said.

She was still pressed against me, and I hastily took a step back.

"Thanks, Cheryl. You do as well."

She pouted at me, and I studied her mouth. Were her lips always that big?

"That's it?" she asked teasingly. "All I get is a 'you look good'?"

"Uh, you look…different," I said.

Cheryl's face twitched, and her eyes squinted up. After a moment, I realized she was trying to frown, but the skin on her forehead remained stubbornly smooth. I watched in fascination as she scrunched her face more, but nothing happened.

"Cheryl, would you be a dear and help Wes get the wine from the kitchen?" my mother said.

"I'd love to," Cheryl said. Her weird mouth turned up in a smile as she slipped her hand into the crook of my elbow. I stared at her hand for a moment before glancing at Daisy. She was staring at us, and unlike Cheryl, I could clearly see the scowl on her face. I wanted to smooth away the cute little lines between her eyes with a kiss, like I was some love-sick jackass in a romantic comedy.

"Wes?" My mother prompted. "The wine, please."

"Right, sorry." Cheryl still clinging to my arm, I left the room.

Once we were in the kitchen, I gave Cheryl a polite smile and eased my arm out of her grip. Before I could open the fridge, she was standing in front of it.

"Uh, I need to get the wine."

"In a minute." She smoothed her now blonde hair with one pale hand. "So, how have you been, Wes?"

"Good," I said.

"I hear you're an engineer now."

"Yes," I said.

She stared expectantly at me, and I said, "How about you? What are you doing?"

"Real estate agent. So, when you're ready to move back home, I'm the girl you can call to find your house." She laughed and crossed both arms over her torso. Her oversized boobs nearly spilled out of her low neckline, and I hastily averted my eyes.

"Oh, I'm not moving back," I said.

"That's a shame," she said. "There are lots of good things about our little town. Did you know when we were kids that I had a huge crush on you?"

I cleared my throat. "Uh, no, I didn't know that."

"I did. Most girls at our high school did. Golden boy Wes, right?"

"Um…" I had no idea what to say. "It was a long time ago."

"Yes, it was," she said. "Some crushes last a long time, though."

"I have a girlfriend," I said. "Back home."

"That's funny, your mom said you were single and had been for quite some time. She told my mother she was really worried about you."

I didn't reply, and Cheryl smiled at me again. Jesus, her teeth were so white. How the hell did she get them that white?

"We could be good together, you know. Why don't we have coffee on Boxing Day? We can get caught up. Afterwards, you could come back to my place, and maybe we can learn some new things about each other."

My jaw dropped. "I'm sorry, are you asking me to…."

Cheryl laughed. "We're both adults here, Wes. Yes, I'm asking you to come back to my house so we can have sex. I'm very attracted to you, and I know that you're attracted to me."

I stared at her in stunned silence, and Cheryl laughed again.

"I know I sound full of myself, but all men are attracted to me now. I have a lot of guys asking me out, Wes. I'm giving you an opportunity here that not many men get. You should take advantage of it while I'm - "

She broke off as Daisy stomped into the room. She looked supremely pissed off, and she glared at me before giving Cheryl a brittle smile. "They're waiting for the wine."

"I'm sorry, who are you?" Cheryl asked.

"She's my girlfriend." Frannie strolled into the kitchen. She put her arm around Daisy's waist and kissed her on the mouth. "Cheryl, meet Daisy Morrison. Daisy, this is an old school friend, Cheryl."

"Girlfriend?" Cheryl eyed Daisy and Frannie for a minute before shrugging. "Not surprised. I always suspected you were a lesbo."

Frannie scowled. "Why does everyone keep saying that?"

"You and Linda Rice were kissing in the art room in eleventh grade," Cheryl replied.

Daisy glanced at Frannie, who shrugged before stepping forward and poking Cheryl in the arm. "Move it, Cheryl. We need the wine."

"Your brother and I are having a private conversation," Cheryl said.

"Yeah, yeah, we heard. You want to bone him on Boxing Day," Frannie replied. "Do me a favour and figure out when the two of you are going to bang when I'm not in hearing range."

She gave Cheryl a little push on the hip, and the woman frowned at her before moving so that Frannie could open the fridge. She pulled out the wine and handed it to Cheryl. "Take this to the dining room, would you?"

Cheryl took the wine before sliding her hand around my arm and leaning against me. "Will you show me where the dining room is, Wesley?"

"Third door on the left," Frannie said.

"Please, Wesley," Cheryl said.

"I'll show you," Daisy said abruptly.

Cheryl glanced at me before sighing. "Fine."

She followed Daisy out of the room as Frannie rolled her eyes and leaned against the counter.

"Holy shit," I said when they were out of earshot. "Does Cheryl look different to you?"

"Yes, you idiot," Frannie laughed. "She's had a shit ton of plastic surgery. I don't think anything about her is real anymore."

"She got a boob job, right?" I said.

"Yeah, and ass implants, a nose job, a chin job, and lip augmentation. Plus, she's got so much Botox in her forehead, she won't be able to frown for at least a decade."

"Thanks for the rescue."

Frannie shrugged. "Wasn't my idea. I think it's hilarious that Mom is trying to set you up with Cheryl, but Daisy insisted on finding out what was taking so long to get the wine. It's her you need to thank."

I would, I thought fervently. The minute I had Daisy alone, she'd know exactly how grateful I was to her for saving me from Cheryl.

I FELT LIKE A CREEPY STALKER AS I FOLLOWED DAISY DOWN THE hallway, but I was desperate to talk to her alone for a moment. She'd been acting weird since the moment the

Bakers arrived. It was bad enough that Mom put me beside Cheryl at dinner, but the clear waves of anger radiating from Daisy were much worse.

She was walking into the bathroom when I caught up to her. I caught the door before she could shut it, and her startled look turned into a scowl. "Excuse me, I need privacy."

"Daisy, we need to talk."

"Do we?" she asked.

"Yes." I stepped into the bathroom and shut the door behind me as she glared at me.

"What are you doing in here? Your entire family and the Bakers are down the hallway," she said in a low voice.

"I don't care," I said.

"Well, I do. Get out of the bathroom," she retorted.

I ignored her anger and pulled her into my arms.

"Hey, let go!"

"Not until you tell me what's wrong," I said. "Why are you angry with me?"

"I'm not angry with you."

"Be truthful, little flower," I said.

She looked away. "So, have you made your plans with Cheryl?"

"What plans?" I asked in confusion.

"Don't be obtuse, Wesley," she said.

"I'm not. I don't have plans with Cheryl."

"Boxing Day," she suddenly snapped. "You're stopping by Cheryl's place for sex. Remember?"

She was jealous. A grin crossed my face. Daisy was jealous of me and Cheryl. She didn't have anything to be jealous about, but holy shit, did it make me feel good that she was.

"Something funny?" she asked.

"You're jealous."

"No, I'm not."

"Yes, you are."

The little angry lines were back between her eyes, and I leaned down and kissed them. "You have nothing to be jealous about, little flower. I'm not interested in Cheryl."

"I leave on Boxing Day," she said.

"I remember."

"Cheryl's very pretty, and it's obvious that she wants you."

"I don't want her. I'm not going to go for coffee with her, let alone go to her house and let her have her dirty way with me."

She stared up at me as relief crossed her face. "Really?"

"Yes," I said. "The only woman who gets to have her dirty way with me is you."

She smiled, and I leaned down and kissed her. She returned my kiss, and I squeezed her ass. "You could have your dirty way with me right now, if you want."

She giggled and shook her head. "We absolutely can't do that, and you know it. In fact," she gave me a gentle push toward the door, "you need to go before we get caught."

I lifted her hand to my mouth and kissed her knuckles. "Sure. Oh, and don't be embarrassed that you're so jealous." I lifted my shirt so she could see my six-pack. The girls always go crazy over me. You'll get used to it after a while."

She rolled her eyes and gave my stomach a hard poke. "Take your ego and go, smartass."

"Yes, ma'am." I gave her one final kiss and left the bathroom. Thankfully, the hallway was still empty, and I headed back to the living room.

CHAPTER 9

Daisy

I stared at the ceiling of the bedroom and listened to Frannie's soft snoring beside me. It was just after midnight, and I was restless and wide awake. I wanted to be with Wes so much it was almost a physical ache. I rolled to my side and stared at the alarm clock, watching as the numbers changed from 12:14 to 12:15.

Well, it was Christmas. The third one without my parents. A wave of homesickness and depression washed over me, and I abruptly slid out of bed and grabbed my phone. Frannie didn't move, and I padded to the door and eased it open before stepping into the hallway. There was a soft glow coming from under Wes's bedroom door, but the rest of the rooms were dark. I held my breath and listened. The house was completely quiet, and I shut Frannie's door and tiptoed to Wes's room. I opened the door and slipped inside.

Wes was sitting up in bed reading a book, and a look of happiness spread across his face. "Hello, gorgeous."

"Why are you still awake?" I asked as I walked across the room.

"Couldn't sleep." He threw back the covers, and I set my phone on the nightstand and crawled into the bed beside him.

"Merry Christmas, Wesley," I said.

"Merry Christmas, little flower." He kissed me, but when I tried to deepen it, he pulled back. "Hold on."

He reached into the nightstand and brought out a small wrapped box. He placed it in my lap, and I smiled at him. "You really didn't have to get me a present."

"I know. Open it."

I untied the ribbon and carefully unwrapped the gift to reveal a plain white box. I opened the lid and gasped in delight. "Oh, Wes. It's beautiful."

I picked up the silk scarf and let it drape over my arm. It was a myriad of different shades of red and absolutely stunning.

"Do you like it?" Wes asked.

"I love it," I said. "Thank you so much."

"You're welcome."

I carefully placed the scarf back into the box, and Wes set it on the floor next to the bed. Wes lay on his back, and I curled on my side next to him. I rested my head against his chest and traced my fingers through his hair as he tugged on my nightdress.

"Take this off."

I sat up and pulled it over my head, then wiggled out of my panties. I ditched them over the side of the bed, blushing a little as Wes's hot gaze roamed over my body.

"Your body is perfect," he said hoarsely.

"Thank you. So is yours." I traced his six-pack as he cupped my breast and teased my nipple into an aching hardness. I leaned over him and we kissed. Slow, deep kisses that made my pulse race and my body tingle.

"You are the best kisser," I panted against his mouth.

He sucked on my bottom lip as his hand pushed between my thighs and cupped my pussy. I pressed my breasts against his chest as he rubbed my clit. I reached down and wrapped my fingers around his cock, stroking him back and forth as he massaged my clit.

"Fuck, that feels good," he muttered.

I was surprised when he reached down and pulled my hand away from his dick. "What's wrong?"

Can I ask you a question?" he said.

"Yes."

"Have you ever given yourself a g-spot orgasm?" His fingers had started up their slow caress of my clit again, and I was finding it difficult to concentrate.

"I tried," I said. "I looked for it a few times, but it remains elusive. I probably don't have one."

Wes grinned at me. "Why don't we find out?"

I glanced at his closed bedroom door. "I've heard they can be pretty intense. What if you do find it and your family hears me…"

Wes wiggled his eyebrows at me. "You'll have to hold in your 'Wes is a sex god' screams."

I laughed, and he kissed my collarbone. "I really want to do this for you, Daisy."

"Okay."

"Lie on your back," he said.

I relaxed on my back as Wes rolled on a condom before lying on his side next to me. I moaned when he leaned over and sucked my nipple into his mouth. He gave it a sharp little nip, and I jerked against him before moaning again. His tongue was already laving away the sting. I wound my fingers in his hair as he sucked and nibbled both my nipples. His fingers were back on my clit, and I moved my hips in slow, tight circles against them.

"Let's see if I can find it this way first," he murmured.

His fingers pushed into me as he lifted his head and stared at my face. He curled his fingers and made a 'come here' motion. Feeling a little self-conscious, I said, "I tried that. It didn't really work, so I don't know if – oh God!"

Wes' fingers had pressed against a spot that made me feel like I was going to pee. He continued to press firmly, and I was reaching for his hand to stop him when the need to pee changed.

"Oh," I whispered. Pleasure was flooding my nervous system, and as Wes pressed and released, I clutched at his arms and gave him a desperate look. "Oh my God, that – that feels so…"

Mere words couldn't describe how it felt. My body was beginning to shake against Wes, and I spread my legs shamelessly wide. The pleasure was growing more intense, and I panted and moaned and made soft pleading noises.

When Wes stopped abruptly, a whine of displeasure exploded from my throat. I clawed at his chest. "Don't you dare fucking stop, Wesley!"

"Shh, little flower." He knelt between my legs. "I want to try something."

"No," I said frantically as he lifted my legs and draped them over his shoulders. "No, I don't want to try something. I want you to keep doing that."

He didn't even flinch when I smacked him in the stomach. "Be nice, Daisy."

"You be nice!" I said in a harsh whisper as he pressed his cock against my opening. "You be nice or I'll…ohhh."

Wes had entered me with one hard thrust, and I clenched around him. It felt good, it really did, but I wanted more than his dick. I'd been so close to the most amazing orgasm of my life, and I was irrationally angry at Wes for taking it away from me.

"Wes! Please!"

"Shh," he whispered again. He adjusted my legs and then pushed into me again. This time, the head of his cock pressed against the same magical spot as his fingers. I barely had time to clamp my hand over my mouth to muffle my shriek of pleasure.

"Good," Wes said.

He held my thighs and thrust in and out with hard pumps of his hips. Each stroke put delicious pressure on my g-spot, and it took less than thirty seconds before the pleasure crested and I was screaming into my hand and writhing under Wes. My climax rolled through me like nothing I'd ever felt before. Wave after wave of intense pleasure washed over me, and I squeezed my inner walls around Wes's dick as my orgasm went on and on.

Wes made a muffled groan and pushed in so deep that I felt the strain in my thigh muscles. He muttered my name as he climaxed, pumping his hips back and forth as the last of my own climax shuddered through me. He pulled out and grabbed my legs when they slipped off his shoulders. I was quivering and shaking, and he rubbed my flat stomach before disposing of the condom and lying on his side next to me.

He rubbed the trembling muscles in my stomach again. "You okay?"

"Marry me," I gasped out.

He laughed and kissed my damp shoulder. "That good, huh?"

"Wes, it was incredible," I whispered. "You have no idea. My orgasm went on and on. I've never felt anything like it before."

"Good, little flower," he said. He rested his head on the pillow beside my head and linked our fingers together.

"Was it okay for you?" I asked.

"Amazing," he said. "Your pussy squeezes me like a vise when you're having a g-spot orgasm. I wanted to last longer, but I didn't stand a chance."

I giggled, and he kissed my cheek before falling silent. I stared at the way our fingers were interlocked, and when my pulse finally slowed to a normal rate, I said, "I feel guilty."

Wes's hand squeezed mine. "About sleeping with me?"

"God no," I said. "But I feel guilty about lying to your family. They're all really nice and so accepting of me, and I'm lying to them."

Wes pulled me into his embrace, and I rested my head on his chest as he rubbed my back. "It was Frannie's idea."

"Yeah, but I agreed to it," I said. "I wish she would tell your family about Owen. Then maybe you and I could - "

I stopped before I could really freak Wes out. As much as I liked Wes, I suddenly had a bad case of cold feet. Just because we were good in bed together didn't mean that we should date. I knew hardly anything about him.

Yeah, it's why you date a person, you idiot.

Good point.

"We could what?" Wes asked.

"Uh, nothing," I said.

He laughed and pulled me a little tighter against his warm body. "Have you ever tried long-distance dating?"

I squinted at him. It was too dark in his room to see his face clearly. I said, "No. Have you?"

"Yes. It kind of sucks, but it can be worth it for the right person."

I tried to sound casual. "Oh yeah?"

"Yeah," he said. "I think we could make it work. Do you?"

Holy shit. Was he serious? My pulse was pounding in my ears, and excitement zinged along my veins.

"Sorry," Wes said suddenly. "Forget I said that. I was reading the room wrong."

I threw my arm around his waist and squeezed him hard. "You're not reading the room wrong. I was a little surprised that's all. I want to date you, Wes."

"Good," he said.

He kissed me, and I rubbed my naked breasts against his chest. He groaned and reached down to cup my ass, kneading it as we kissed with slow brushes of our lips and tongues.

When he pulled back, I rubbed his hip and said, "I'm unemployed."

"I like to play Dungeons and Dragons," Wes said as he cupped my breast.

I blinked at him. "What?"

"Are we not playing a game of 'say the least sexy thing in bed you can think of and see if the other one is still turned on'?" Wes asked. "Just so you know, I still think you're hot even without a job."

I laughed so hard that Wes pulled the covers over my head to muffle the sound. I poked my head out and gave him a mock scowl. "I'm not playing a sex game with you, Wesley. I was only pointing out that I'm unemployed, single and not particularly attached to the city I currently live in."

Wes's hand squeezed my hip. "Would you seriously consider moving to my city?"

I nodded. "Yes. If I found a job there."

"That's fucking fantastic!"

"Shh!" I said with a nervous look at the door. "Keep your voice down."

"Right, sorry," he said. "Listen, don't feel pressured to move. I mean, I want you to consider it, but I don't want you to feel like you have to."

"I don't," I said. "I would move because I want to. I'd like to get the chance to know you better."

"So, this means your vow of celibacy is officially over,

yeah?" Wes said with a slight grin.

"I don't know," I said. "That Dungeons and Dragons revelation has me seriously considering a life of celibacy again."

"Hey, Dungeons and Dragons is sexy."

"Is it, though?"

"No," Wes said sadly. "No, it really isn't."

I laughed and threw my thigh over his before tracing my fingers over his flat abdomen. "I bet another orgasm would help me forget you're a role-playing game nerd. Why don't you show me what else those fingers can do besides rolling some dice?"

"Yes, ma'am," Wes said with a wicked grin.

Wes

"WESLEY? TIME TO GET UP!"

I sat up, my heart pounding when the door opened and my mother walked into my room. I could still feel Daisy's soft warmth behind me, and I prayed feverishly that she would stay where she was. It went unanswered. She sat up and stared sleepily at me. "Wes? What's wrong?"

"Oh, Wesley," my mother said.

Daisy made a small shriek and yanked the covers to her chest as my mother pressed her lips together. "Oh, Wesley. What have you done?"

"It's my fault," Daisy said immediately. "Patricia, all of this is my fault, and I can explain."

"Why would you do this to Frannie?" Mom asked.

"Do what?" My grandmother wandered into the room, and I groaned as her eyes nearly bulged out of her head. "Holy shit! Wesley, are you having sex with your sister's lesbian girlfriend?"

"What is Wesley doing?" Dad yelled down the hallway.

"He's having sex with his sister's lesbian lover!" Grandma shouted back.

"He's what?"

"He's having sex with Daisy! She must be bisexual!" Grandma hollered.

My father appeared in the doorway. "She's what?"

"Bisexual," my grandmother said. "It means she likes to screw men and women."

"I know what it means, Mother!" Dad retorted. "Wes, you should be ashamed of yourself."

"Everybody out of my room," I said. "Let us get dressed and we'll explain - "

"What's going on?" Her hair sticking up and rubbing her eyes, Frannie appeared in the doorway next to my father. She yawned. "Why is everyone yelling?"

"Frannie, honey, I'm so sorry," my mother said.

"Sorry about what? Why are we all standing in Wes's room... what the hell?" Frannie's eyes got wide, and she stared at Daisy and me. "Daisy? You're... sleeping with Wes?"

"Frannie, I..." Daisy trailed off and gave me a look of misery.

I took her hand and squeezed it before staring at my sister. "Tell them the truth, Frannie."

Frannie's face paled, and she glanced at my parents.

"What is he talking about?" Dad asked.

"Tell them, Frannie," I said.

Frannie took a deep breath, and I scowled when big crocodile tears dripped down her face. "I can't believe my own brother would betray me like this! I was in love with her, you asshole!"

She burst into wailing sobs and ran from the room. My father and grandmother both went after her as Mom stared silently at us.

"Mom, she's faking," I said. "She's not in love with Daisy. She's in love with - "

"Stop it, Wesley," my mom said. "I am so disappointed in you." Her gaze moved to Daisy. "Disappointed in both of you. Shame on both of you for breaking Frannie's heart."

Daisy made a low, sobbing gasp as my mother left the room and shut the door behind her.

"It's okay, darlin'," I said.

"It isn't," she sobbed. "This is all my fault. I forgot to set my alarm on my phone last night. If I hadn't, we wouldn't have slept in."

"It'll be fine," I said. "Frannie will tell them the truth."

"No, she won't," Daisy said as tears ran down her face. "You know she won't, Wes. She's terrified your father will find out and be angry with her."

"Then we'll tell them."

"Like they'll believe us," Daisy whispered.

I cursed under my breath. "Get dressed, Daisy. I'll meet you downstairs, okay?"

She nodded, and I kissed her before wiping at the tears on her cheeks. "Don't cry. I'm going to fix this, I promise."

Daisy

I TOOK LONGER THAN USUAL TO GET DRESSED. MY STOMACH was churning, and I kept seeing the look on Patricia's face when she said she was disappointed in me. I had ruined their Christmas, and despite what Wes said, I knew Frannie would never admit to dating Owen.

I took a deep breath and started downstairs. I had heard Wes go downstairs five minutes ago, and it wasn't fair of me to leave him alone to deal with his family. I could hear

Frannie crying in the living room and, my legs trembling, I walked into the room.

Wes was nowhere in sight, and my stomach dropped as Frannie's parents stared at me. Frannie was still crying steadily on the couch between them, and her mother rubbed her back. "There, there, Frannie. It'll be all right, dearest."

"Frannie," I said. "You need to tell them the truth."

I had no idea why Wes had abandoned me to face his family alone, but I couldn't really blame him.

"You're one to talk about telling the truth," Gregory snapped. "I think you need to leave."

"Dad, no! You are not kicking Daisy out." Frannie gave him a horrified look.

"Greg, it's Christmas Day," Patricia said.

"I don't care," Gregory said. "She needs to leave my house right now."

"Mom, Dad, listen to me," Frannie said urgently. "There's something you need to know. There's this boy and…oh God, this is so hard to tell you."

"What are you talking about?" Patricia said as the front door opened.

"You cannot drag my son out of our home on Christmas morning! Let him go right now, or I swear I will call the police!" The angry voice of Ryan Brenner bellowed through the house.

Gregory jumped up from the couch as Wes marched into the living room. He had Owen by the arm, and Mr. and Mrs. Brenner were right behind them.

"What the hell are you doing in my house, Brenner?" Gregory snarled.

"Ask your son!" Ryan shouted. "He's the one who dragged Owen over here. He's gone insane, and I'm charging him with assault."

"Dad, chill out," Owen said. "God, dude, you're gonna

have a stroke. You've really gotta…"

He trailed off as he caught sight of Frannie sitting on the couch. "Babe? Oh my God! Babe, what's wrong? Why are you crying?"

He shook loose of Wes and ran across the room to kneel at Frannie's feet. He cupped her face and pressed his mouth against hers. "Babe, tell me why you're sad."

"I'm sorry, baby," Frannie cried. "We have to tell them. They're going to kick Daisy out of the house."

"It's fine, Frannie." Owen sat beside Frannie and put his arm around her shoulders. "I love you, and I want them to know."

Patricia stood and walked over to Gregory as Wes put his arm around my waist and pulled me up against him. Gregory was staring at Frannie and Owen, and when Patricia put her arm around him, he said, "Patty? Why is our lesbian daughter kissing Owen Brenner in our living room?"

"Love, sit down. You're pale," Patricia said.

Gregory shook his head. Two spots of red were appearing in his cheeks. "No, I want to know what's going on."

"Isn't it obvious?" Frannie's grandmother said. "Your daughter is bisexual. She's screwing Owen and Daisy, and Daisy is screwing Frannie and Wes. It's like a damn soap opera."

The old woman smiled gleefully at everyone. "This is the best Christmas ever."

"I'm not bisexual, Grandma," Frannie said, "and neither is Daisy. Owen and I have been dating for over a year, but I was too afraid to tell Dad, so I asked Daisy to pretend to be my girlfriend. I didn't want you guys to try to set me up with other men during the entire holiday. None of this is Daisy's fault. She was doing me a favour."

"Oh, Frannie. You should have told us the truth," Patricia said. "We don't care who you date, we just want you to be happy. Isn't that right, Gregory?"

He didn't reply, and Patricia elbowed him sharply. "Gregory! Isn't that right?"

"Yes," Gregory sighed.

"Well, we're not okay with it," Owen's father said. "No son of ours is going to date Gregory McKinley's daughter. Owen, you get your ass off that couch and away from that girl right now. You're too good for her."

"Ryan," Mrs. Brenner said. "Stop speaking for me. I don't - "

"Too good for my daughter? That's rich, coming from a guy whose son works at a Best Buy," Gregory snapped.

"He's a manager," Ryan shouted. "At least my son doesn't lie to my face like your daughter."

"You watch your mouth, Brenner. She only lied because she knew what an asshole you are," Gregory said.

"I'm the asshole? You know, I've had just about enough of you and your family. You've always thought you're better than us and - "

"I don't think I'm better than you! I know I'm better than you!"

"All these years and you still think that you're - "

"ENOUGH!"

Patricia's voice shouted above the voices of the arguing men. I was so shocked to hear the soft-spoken Patricia yelling that I jerked against Wes and gave him a look of alarm. He returned my look before taking a step back, pulling me with him, as Patricia stalked by us.

"Both of you need to quit acting like immature assholes," Patricia said as she glared at Gregory and Ryan. "This stupid feud of yours has gone on long enough. For God's sake, Joy and I have been friends for over twenty years!"

Ryan turned to his wife. "Joy?"

"It's true," Mrs. Brenner said. "We are."

"Wha- how?" Gregory sputtered.

"We live right next door to each other, and we were both stay-at-home moms," Patricia said. "We became friends when the kids were little. You know my monthly Friday night bridge game?"

Gregory nodded slowly, and Patricia grinned at Joy. "It's actually my movie night with Joy. We have dinner, go to a movie, and talk about how ridiculous our husbands' feud is."

"We text every day," Joy said.

"This can't be happening," Ryan said.

He staggered on his feet, and Owen jumped up to cross the room and take his arm. "Sit down, Dad."

"It's happening, Ryan," Joy said when he was sitting in the armchair. "Patricia and I are friends, and now our children are dating. Get used to it."

"I don't want to," Ryan said.

"I don't care," Joy said. "In fact," she glanced at Patricia, "Patty, why don't we all have Christmas dinner together this year?"

"No!" Ryan and Gregory said in unison.

"I think that's a wonderful idea," Patricia said. "I'm sure Owen and Frannie want to spend Christmas together. Why don't you come back around three? We're eating at four."

"We'll be here," Joy said. "I'll bring over our turkey as well. It's already in the oven."

"Perfect," Patricia said. "Owen, honey, you're welcome to stay while we open up presents, if you'd like."

"Nah, that's okay," Owen said. "You do your family thing. I'll see my lady in a few hours."

He pressed another kiss against Frannie's mouth. "See you soon."

"I love you, Owen," Frannie said.

"Love you too, babe," Owen said.

Gregory grimaced, and Ryan made a sound of disgust, but

they both kept their mouths shut as Owen stood and ambled toward the doorway. After a moment, Mr. and Mrs. Brenner followed him. When the front door shut, Wes pressed a kiss against my forehead.

"You okay, little flower?"

"Yes," I said, "are you?"

He nodded before bending his head and kissing me on the mouth.

"Gross."

He pulled back and glared at his sister. "Shut up, Frannie."

"How long have you two been banging?" she asked.

"Francine," Patricia said. "Don't be rude."

"Sorry, Mom," Frannie said.

Patricia approached us and gave us both a rueful smile. "I'm sorry for what I said."

I shook my head. "No, it's fine. You didn't know, and I know how bad it looked when you found me in Wes's bed. But I want you to know that Frannie is my best friend and I would never purposely hurt her, and I really like your son."

She smiled at me before reaching up to pat Wes's cheek. "He really likes you, too, I can tell."

"I knew it," Frannie's grandmother said to us. "I knew you two were going at it like bunnies."

"Mother, please," Gregory said wearily. "Not now, okay?"

"Coffee. Let's make some coffee, and then we'll open presents," Patricia said briskly. "Gregory, Mother Francine, come with me, please."

As they left the living room, we heard Gregory say, "Are you really friends with Brenner's wife?"

Wes laughed. "I think Dad's more upset that Mom is friends with Mrs. Brenner than he is about Frannie dating Owen."

Frannie stood up from the couch. "So, how long have you been banging?"

Wes rolled his eyes. "None of your business."

His sister suddenly froze before giving me a suspicious look. "Oh my God. Was Wes your one-night stand, our first night here?"

My cheeks turned red and I nodded. "Yeah, I didn't know he was your brother, Frannie. I swear. I met him at the bar, and we didn't exchange last names or anything. Then, when he walked into the kitchen the next day…"

Frannie made a retching noise. "Oh God, now I have a mental image of you two having sex. That's so gross."

"Not gross at all," Wes said cheerfully.

"Why were you in Wes's room last night?" she asked.

"She's been in my room every night," Wes said, "because you kicked her out so you could have sex with Owen."

"I told her to go to the basement bedroom," Frannie said.

"Like she could make it past Mom," Wes said. "Honestly, you're the reason we're dating."

"You're dating?" Frannie said in surprise. "You don't even live in the same city."

Wes glanced at me, and Frannie said, "Oh goddammit, Wes. You convinced her to move, didn't you?"

"No," I said. "I brought up the idea of moving."

Frannie sighed. "Well, I'm grossed out that you're sleeping with my brother and sad that you're leaving me, but I guess whatever makes you happy and shit."

I laughed. "I love you too, Frannie."

She gave us an apologetic look. "I'm sorry that I pretended to be the jilted lover."

"That was a dick move," I said.

"I panicked, but I should have confessed immediately," Frannie said.

"I'll forgive you, but the next time our ruse of fake lesbianism is discovered, you have to tell the truth immediately."

"There isn't going to be a next time," Wes said. "From now on, I'm the only one who kisses you, Daisy."

"God, Wes. Possessive much?" Frannie hugged me. "Love you, honey. I'm gonna grab some coffee."

She left the living room, and Wes tugged me back into his embrace. "See, I told you it would be fine, little flower."

I smiled at him. "So, now that your family knows about us, does this mean I should officially start looking for a job in your city, Mr. McKinley?"

"I think that's a brilliant idea, Ms. Morrison," Wes said.

He pressed a kiss against my mouth. "Merry Christmas, Daisy."

"Merry Christmas, Wes."

EPILOGUE

Two years later

Daisy

"Daisy! Hello, dearest. Come in out of the cold!" Patricia pulled me into the house and hugged me. "Where's Wes?"

"Grabbing the suitcases from the car." I took off my jacket and hung it up before following Patricia into the kitchen. "Are Frannie and Owen here yet?"

"They are, but they're at the Brenners. I swear this might be the Christmas that starts up Gregory and Ryan's feud again," she said. "Although fighting over who gets to hold their new granddaughter is a legitimate reason to bring it back to life."

I laughed as Wes walked into the kitchen. He hugged his mom, and she kissed his cheek. "Hi, dearest. How was the trip?"

"Fine. We had a bit of trouble with the car rental place at

the airport, but we managed to get it sorted out. Where's Dad?"

"In the basement. Why?"

Wes wiggled his eyebrows at her before leaving the kitchen. I heard him yelling for his Dad as his grandmother walked into the kitchen.

"Hello, Daisy."

"Hello, Grandma Francine. How are you?" I stood and hugged the fragile old woman.

"Can't complain," she said. She suddenly blinked and grabbed my left hand. She stared at the ring on my finger as Patricia pulled a pan of cookies from the stove.

"I swear, this is the warmest Christmas we've had in years. We won't need our winter jackets when we get the tree tomorrow," Patricia said.

I put my finger to my lips and winked at Wes' grandmother. Her wrinkled face lit up, and she made a zipping motion across her mouth before sitting down next to me. "Where's my great-grandbaby?"

"They're still at Joy and Ryan's," Patricia said. "They should be here any minute, though."

"Mom?" The front door slammed as Frannie's voice carried down the hall. "We're back."

"In the kitchen, dearest," Patricia shouted.

I turned in anticipation as Frannie and Owen walked into the kitchen. Owen was holding the car seat, and he set it on the floor in front of me before kissing my cheek. "Hey, Daisy."

"Hi, Owen." I was already reaching into the car seat, and I unbuckled the tiny baby before lifting her into my arms. "Hello, sweetheart. Your Aunt Daisy misses you so much."

"She misses you, too. One quick visit when she was born isn't enough." Frannie sat down beside me and watched as I placed the baby on my shoulder and rubbed her back. "In fact, she misses you so much that she insists you do the nighttime feedings."

I laughed. "I'm more than happy to help, Frannie."

"God, I love you. Are you sure you don't want to move back and live with me and Owen?"

"So, she can be your unpaid nanny?" Wes walked into the room. His dad was with him, and I grinned when Gregory's face lit up and he hurried over. I handed the baby to him, and he kissed her forehead.

Frannie scowled at Wes. "Better than living with you. She figured out you wear your underwear more than once, yet?"

"Hey, I quit doing that when I turned fifteen," Wes said as I made a face.

He laughed and kissed my forehead. "So, did you tell Frannie already?"

"No," I said.

"Tell me what?" Frannie asked.

Wes pulled me to my feet and put his arm around me. "I asked Daisy to marry me and she said yes."

"What?" Frannie shrieked. She stood and grabbed my hand, staring wide-eyed at the ring as Patricia clapped excitedly and hugged Wes.

Frannie studied my ring for a moment before pulling me into her embrace. "Congratulations, Oopsie. I'm so happy for you!"

"Thank you, Frannie," I replied.

She stepped back as the other members of Wes' family crowded around me to say congratulations and look at the ring.

"What a wonderful surprise," Patricia said. She wiped at the tears on her face before hugging me hard. "I'm so glad you're a part of our family, dearest."

"I am too," I said. I returned her hug and then hugged Gregory, Owen, and Wes's grandmother. The baby let out a sharp cry, and I couldn't help but smile as everyone rushed to Gregory's side and began fussing over her.

Wes put his arm around me and kissed my neck. "Well, we had five minutes of glory before my niece stole the show again."

"I don't mind," I said. "I love you, Wes."

"I love you too, little flower."

Looking for more Christmasy goodness? Keep reading for an excerpt of The Christmas Nanny.

THE CHRISTMAS NANNY
EXCERPT

All I want for Christmas is my next door neighbour.

Widower Sam Black isn't looking for love.

It doesn't matter how gorgeous, funny, or tempting his neighbour is. Tess is not his priority. His son is.

But he and Oscar have been burned before.

When Oscar's nanny quits unexpectedly, he'll need a babysitter over Christmas break. Will the recently unemployed Tess be the perfect solution?

Fulfilling her dream of becoming a vet technician requires money, and Tess can't turn down the sexy single dad next door when he asks her to babysit. Turns out, spending extra time with Sam is better than double overtime.

As she and Sam grow closer, Tess imagines a life with him and Oscar. But Sam's been hurt before, and he's made it clear he isn't looking for anything serious.

Can Tess's love, Oscar's infatuation, and the magic of Christmas change Sam's mind? Or will Sam's emotional scars keep him from accepting that Tess is the missing piece to his little family?

Tess

I watched the black and white cat wind its way around Sam's lower legs. He reached down and stroked its back. It arched and purred and rubbed against him again. As I watched his long fingers rub the side of the cat's face, I decided it was much too weird that I wished I were the damn cat.

I concentrated on the little orange tabby I held. Her name was Marmalade, she was fourteen months old, and I was already completely smitten with her. We had walked into the cat room at the humane society, and I thought Oscar would lose his mind with excitement. Cats of all colours and ages wandered freely around the room. Some were sitting or sleeping in the oversized, overstuffed, and clawed-up armchairs, while others perched on the multiple scratching posts scattered around the room. Some had curled up in the empty cardboard boxes or cat beds placed in various spots in the room.

Three volunteers were in the room, and I wasn't at all surprised when one of them made an immediate beeline for Sam. She had latched onto him with the fierceness of a winter storm, but I couldn't blame her. He was damn hot. It was unsettling to feel jealousy stir in my stomach, though, when she touched his arm, giggled, and flirted. I was mollified by the fact that Sam seemed immune to her flirting. Either he was oblivious to her flirting, or he wasn't into blonde women with amazing curves.

He knew she was flirting with him. Maybe he prefers dark-haired women with slender bodies.

Yeah, maybe. I turned my attention back to Marmalade when she butted my chin with her forehead. She purred loudly as I scratched her throat.

"She's cute."

Sam suddenly stood next to me, and I had to stop myself from leaning into his body. God, he smelled good. I don't know what aftershave he used, but it smelled delicious. I shifted Marmalade in my arms and tried to ignore the way my girlie parts were starting to tingle.

"I like her," I said.

"So, she's the one?" he asked.

"She's the one."

"That's great."

He reached out to pet Marmalade just as I did, and our fingers brushed. He immediately jerked his hand away, and I tried not to let my disappointment show. It was only a brief touch, but butterflies had swarmed to life in my stomach, and I was suddenly much too warm.

"Sorry," I said.

"My fault," he said before searching the room for Oscar. "Oscar? Buddy, it's time to go."

"Daddy! I found a kitten for Tess," Oscar said from behind us.

We turned, and my jaw dropped as Sam made a croaking sound of surprise. Oscar held a large, grey, long-haired cat around the middle of its body. Its front paws draped over Oscar's shoulders, and its fluffy tail dragged along the ground as Oscar smiled happily at us. Despite the awkward way Oscar held it, the cat lounged contentedly against him.

"Is that cat missing a leg?" Sam said.

"And an eye," I said.

"What the…"

Sam trailed off as the cat turned its head to stare at us. The sunken socket where his left eye used to be was more than a little disturbing. His muzzle was covered in pale scars, and a big chunk was missing from his nose. His right eye, a bright green orb of colour, studied us for a moment before judging us lacking. He turned his gaze to Oscar, and the little boy giggled when the cat licked his chin with his scratchy tongue.

"He likes me, Daddy!"

"Oscar, buddy, Tess has already -"

"Do you like him, Tess?" Oscar asked eagerly. "The lady said his name is One-Eyed Jack and he's been here a really long time."

"I can't imagine why," Sam muttered into my ear.

I tried not to laugh as one of the volunteers approached us and said, "How are we doing? Need any help?"

"We want this one!" Oscar said.

"Buddy, no," Sam said. "Tess has already picked out her kitten."

Oscar studied the orange cat in my arms. "But I like One Eyed Jack."

"It's Tess who's getting the cat, remember?" Sam said.

Oscar's face drew down into a pout, and he held the big grey cat a little tighter. "But Jack likes me."

"I know he looks a bit rough," the volunteer said, "but Jack is actually a great cat. He's very laid back, and he likes other cats, so he and Marmalade would get along just fine."

"My landlord is only allowing me to have one cat," I said.

I stared at Oscar's sweet face, torn between my desire to have Marmalade and my desire not to hurt Oscar's feelings.

"Tess," Oscar said, "why don't you like Jack?"

"It isn't that she doesn't like him," Sam said. "It's just that she also likes Marmalade. Marmalade will be a better cat for Tess than Jack. Besides, Jack will find a new home, won't he?"

He gave the volunteer a pointed look. She nodded. "He

sure will. In fact, if no one takes him home tonight, tomorrow he's going to a beautiful farm."

"He is?" Oscar said.

"Yes," the volunteer said. "There are lots of other cats to play with and fields of catnip for him to roll in. He'll be very happy."

Oh God, I was getting a bad feeling in the pit of my stomach. I stared at Sam. He looked as alarmed as I felt.

As Oscar buried his face in Jack's fur, Sam said to the volunteer, "Are you saying what I think you're saying?"

The volunteer nodded. "We have a lot of cats right now and not enough room. Jack's old, and most people are grossed out by the missing leg, eye, and scars."

"So, tomorrow One-Eyed Jack's going to be…" I couldn't say it.

"One-Eyed Jack will be walking with Jesus tomorrow," the volunteer said in a cheerful voice. "Now, let me get the paperwork started for Marmalade."

As she walked away, I stared wide-eyed at Sam. "Sam…"

He studied Oscar and the old grey cat before staring at me. "Well, shit."

ABOUT THE AUTHOR

Elizabeth Kelly was born and raised in Ontario, Canada. She moved west as a teenager and now lives in Alberta with her husband and a menagerie of pets. She firmly believes that a person can survive solely on sushi and coffee, and only her husband's mad cooking skills prevents her from proving that theory.

For more information about Elizabeth, check out her website at

www.elizabethkelly.ca

facebook.com/EKellyBooks
instagram.com/elizabethkelly_author
amazon.com/Elizabeth-Kelly/e/B00EOHZ0MS
bookbub.com/authors/elizabeth-kelly
bsky.app/profile/elizabethkelly.bsky.social
threads.net/@elizabethkelly_author

Porter's Mate (Book Four)

Bria and the Tiger (Book Five)

Rosalie Undone (Book Six)

The Dragon's Mate (Book Seven)

Rise of the Jaguar (Book Eight)

The Assassin and the Bear (Book Nine)

Elora and the Crow (Book Ten)

The Draax Series

Reign (Book One)

Rule (Book Two)

Rebel (Book Three)

Surrender (Book Four)

Survive (Book Five)

Salvation (Book Six)

Harmony Falls Series

Sweet Harmony (Book One)

Perfect Harmony (Book Two)

Forbidden Harmony (Book Three)

Redeeming Harmony (Book Four)

Absolute Harmony (Novella)

Beautiful Harmony (Book Five)

Reckless Harmony (Book Six)

Seasoned Romance Series

Bet Your Heart on Me (Book One)

Take a Chance on Me (Book Two)

Place Your Trust in Me (Book Three)

Individual Books

The Necessary Engagement

Amelia's Touch

The Rancher's Daughter

Healing Gabriel

The Contract

A Home for Lily

Saving Charlotte

Shameless

The Fairy Tales Collection

Broken

Always

An Unlikely Seduction

Holiday Romance

The Christmas Wife

The Christmas Rescue

The Christmas Nanny

The Christmas Boss

Sordid Games